Gods of Arcadia Origins
Book 2

The
Academy

Andrea Stehle

The Gods of Arcadia

Long ago the Olympian gods lived among the mortals of Earth. It was a time of menacing monsters and heroic deeds. Olympians and mortals lived in a chaotic world without rules or consequences. It was the age of mythology, but it could not endure.

The Olympians were careless and let mankind escape from their influence. There were too many mortals with too many new ideas to control. No matter how hard they tried, the Olympians discovered they could not stop the progress of human history. So, they took the only option left to them – they started over.

Transplanting a small group of human colonists to the distant world of Arcadia, they created a new mythical world. This time it would be perfect. Arcadia would be a world where Olympians rule and mortals obey. Arcadia would be a world where the future and the past could live side by side.

To promote harmony, the Great Law of the Olympians forbids all war on Arcadia. For two thousand years. the Gods and mortals have lived in harmony, although even the Olympians would have to admit - nothing is ever perfect.

Arcadian Calendar

Season	Name of Month
Fall	Dionysus
Fall	Hera
Fall	Demeter
Winter	Hermes
Winter	Hephaestus
Spring	Apollo
Spring	Artemis
Spring	Aphrodite
Summer	Athena
Summer	Poseidon
Summer	Hera

Forward

Queen Lyessa is considered by most historians to be one of the most important rulers Amazonia has ever known. The journal of her visit to New Athens and her days at the Academy give us glimpses into the woman and queen she would someday become.

Lady Ardella of New Athens is a figure know well by history. She was chosen by the Goddess Athena and entrusted with power at a very young age, but in the pages of this diary she is just one of many students at the Academy. It is a fascinating glimpse of who Ardella was before she became the Daughter of Athena.

Either document alone would be valuable to historians, but together they record the forging of the friendship between these two powerful women as young girls. This historian believes that the bond that developed between Ardella and Lyessa changed the history of Arcadia forever.

Denarian Strom
Professor of History at the Academy
Two thousand, six hundred and ninety-eight years
Ab Terra Condita

This book is dedicated to my friend and
fellow educator, Jennifer Friedrich
whose life touched so many.

We will miss you.

Chapter 1
From the journal of Lyessa, princess of the Amazons

The 1st day of the month of Athena
Two thousand six hundred and thirty years Ab Terra Condita

I have arrived safely in New Athens, although I still haven't seen the Academy where I will spend the next three months of my life. I'm staying with Ardella's family for a few days until it is time for classes to begin.

They have been very kind to me, especially Ardella's mother Lady Lucinda. Their guest room is nice and the bed is comfortable, but I am finding it hard to fall asleep.

I'm sure my sister Anna would say it is the strangeness of a new place making me too restless to sleep. I would be quick to point out that I had no problem sleeping on the hard ground of Mt. Orion during my survival training – even with silver lupines howling in the distance.

So why would a soft bed make me edgy just because it was in the city of another Olympian? Whatever the reason I can't sleep, it is chance to write my first journal entry in New Athens.

The city of the Goddess Athena is not exactly what I expected. Ardella and I spent the last few hours of the two day trip up on the observation deck hoping to get a better view the city as we approached.

It seemed like we had been waiting there forever (in fact Ardella had just fallen asleep) when we came over a low hill and the city was suddenly right in front of us.

I had heard many stories about the Tower of Athena. It was over sixty floors of marble and stone that was not only the home of the patron goddess of New Athens, but a building which housed one copy of every book ever written by the human race since our days on ancient Earth.

For some reason, I assumed that any building that important would loom over the rest of the city. Instead it was part of a collection of skyscrapers similar to the image Ardella once showed me of a place called New York City.

Unlike Athena's classic marble tower, however, all the other skyscrapers were made of metal and glass. They came in every size and shape imaginable and formed a strange sort of artificial landscape, so unlike Amazonia that I wondered both places could be found on the same planet.

The sun was just setting as we arrived in New Athens and I watch amazed as the lights of the city changed the skyline into a twinkling forest of green, blue, and red boxes floating in the night.

The sight was so stunning that it took my breath away. I was an Amazon very far from home. A single tear slipped down my cheek. It tasted salty on my lips. Looking back – I am not sure if it was a tear of joy or a tear of sorrow.

Although my first glimpse of New Athens was more than I had expected, my first encounter with a boy was a little disappointing. Ardella's brother Rafe stood blocking the hall, as we wearily made our way toward our bedrooms.

He had the same brown hair as Ardella, and was quite a bit taller than his twin sister. Instead of Ardella's warm brown eyes, his deep blue ones flashed like the waters of Lake Hera in the noonday sun. That was especially true when he made it clear he was unhappy with his sister's return.

"You're finally home," he scoffed. "I thought you might have decided to stay and join an Amazon training cohort."

"I'm too tired to deal with you tonight, Rafe. It was a very long trip home. I am going to bed. Lysi, I'll see you in the morning."

"Goodnight, Ardella," I replied.

Suddenly I found myself alone in the hall with Rafe, and just a little nervous. *What did you say to a boy?*

"You must be the stray Mother brought home from her trip. You don't look like an Amazon. You look just like all my sister's silly friends."

Rafe's eyes flashed with anger, and I wondered how he could be so hostile to someone he just met. I had done nothing to deserve this treatment.

I suspected he was trying to goad me into a verbal contest, and I should just ignore his comment. Unfortunately for Ardella's brother, the Amazon in me could not pass up such a challenge.

"What would a boy from New Athens know about Amazons?" I asked with just enough sarcasm to let him know what I thought of his rude behavior.

He smirked at me.

"You think you're better than me, just because you're a girl."

I shook my head at this strange person called a boy and told him the truth.

"Although I am not terribly impressed with you at the moment, I really have no way to judge. You are the first boy I have ever met."

"Because boys aren't allowed in Amazonia. Mother took Ardella on her trip, because the Amazons wouldn't even allow me to visit your island."

Finally, I understood to cause of his anger. Ardella had told me her brother was the adventurer in the family, and had been upset that he was not allowed to come on the trip to Amazonia.

Apparently, his anger had been simmering all this time awaiting his sister's return. Since she had refused to take the bait, he had turned his frustration towards me.

Although I had little hope it would pacify him, I decided a lesson on Amazons was called for in this moment.

"All Hera's followers are women. That is how the Goddess wishes it."

"Just like all the members of Athena's Council are women, because that is how the Goddess wishes it."

That was an interesting observation. I had always been taught that Hera was the only one on Arcadia with a matriarchal society. But even in New Athens where there are both men and women lived - women had an advantage, since their patron Olympian was a Goddess. *Interesting*.

Of course, there was no reason to let Rafe know he had a valid complaint, so I just replied, "I suppose."

"Just because the Athena says it, doesn't mean girls are better than boys."

"Just because Hera doesn't allow men in her city doesn't prove she the thinks girls are better than boys."

"You just defend Hera because you're a girl."

"And you seem to resent Athena because you are a boy."

"I just want to know why I'm not good enough to visit Amazonia, when Ardella gets to go."

"I don't pretend to speak for Hera or Athena, but I don't think it's personal. We can assume they are a little biased when it comes to gender equality. Neither has shown much interest in men since coming to Arcadia."

He just stared at me for a moment, as if trying to decide how to take my words.

"You're funny."

"I am so glad I could amuse you."

"You're not too bad – for a girl."

"Now who is being biased? You don't even know me, yet you dislike me just because I am a girl."

"Don't take it so personally. I don't like any of Ardella's friends."

"So Ardella warned me."

I realized this discussion was a waste of my time and energy. It was foolish to spend any more time talking.

"Goodnight, Rafe," I said, hoping to put an end to this strange conversation. I was not that lucky.

"Just don't expect special treatment at the Academy. People aren't going to care that you are some Amazon princess."

Annoyed by his comment and the butterflies that suddenly filled my stomach, I pushed past Ardella's brother toward the guestroom.

He couldn't know how nervous I was about being in a new place and attending a new school.

He was just being annoying, until those last words - they hurt. He did that on purpose.

I wonder if all males are so unpleasant. I hope not, since Ardella says they make up half the population at the Academy.

Chapter 2
From the diary of Ardella of New Athens

The 2nd day of the month of Athena
Two thousand six hundred and thirty years Ab Terra Condita

We are finally home. I do not understand why coming back from a trip seems to take longer than getting there did. It makes no logical sense, but it is true. I was so tired last night when we got home; I fell asleep fully dressed on top of my covers. Lyessa laughed when she found me that way this morning.

As we headed to breakfast Lyessa told me about her strange encounter with Rafe last night. I have never understood my twin's obsession with who is better – boys or girls. I have come to expect him to be rude to me, but I felt bad he acted that way towards my new friend.

At least he was nicer to Lyessa with Mother and Father in the room. Although if I were honest about it, he was simply silent as Mother and I answered Father's questions about the trip.

When I asked Rafe what he had been doing while Mother and I were in Amazonia, he just grumbled something about animals. Father had to explain that he had been helping him with the care of the animals.

Father is a zoologist and has been the director of the Academy's Menagerie for many years. Rafe and I had always been too young to help before, but it seems like that has changed. Rafe is so lucky. I hope one day I can help Father with the animals, too.

Mother and Father both had to attend the Faculty Convocation to prepare for the upcoming trimester, so Rafe, Lyessa and I were on our own for the afternoon.

It is the first time I can remember not having an adult around to watch us while they were away. First Rafe gets to help in the animal enclosures and now we were trusted to be on our own all afternoon. We are growing up and our parents have starting to give us more freedom and more responsibility.

It is exciting and scary all at the same time.

After dinner tonight, Mother and I taught Lyessa an ancient Earth game called Dominos. It involves counting and matching dots. Mother had a set of the rectangular playing tiles made for me for my fifth birthday. It is still one of my favorite games.

Having a mother that specialized in ancient Earth history means life is never dull. The archive on "pop culture" is filled with all sorts of strange and interesting games, books, songs, and videos from our ancestors back on Earth. They had incredible imaginations and were a little strange.

The 3rd day of the month of Athena

Mother took Lyessa to the Academy to register for her classes early this morning. I hoped she will be in the same Ancient Earth History course with Mistress Rhianna that I am taking this trimester. Lyessa told me that she wanted to request me as a roommate, since I was the only person at the Academy she knew. I hope the Headmaster allows it.

When they return, Mother says we can take Lyessa into the city to visit one of the museums or to a lecture at the Lyceum. She said I would get to pick where we go. I can't seem to decide if we should go to the Museum of Natural Science, or the Arcadian History Archive, or maybe the Aviary to feed the birds. The best part is Rafe has gone to help Father with the animals in the Menagerie today, so he won't be coming with us.

I can't believe I actually missed him while I was in Amazonia. *How could I have forgotten how annoying he is?*

The 4th day of the month of Athena

I had a strange dream last night – at least I think it was a dream. I woke up uncertain where I was for a few moments. It seemed so real. I know it will fade in my memory quickly, so I must write it down.

I stood on the edge of a marble balcony looking out at the city of New Athens. It had to have been in one of the taller buildings. I was higher up than I had ever been before.

Looking down at sunlight glistening off the mirrored windows of buildings, I could see rainbows bouncing back and forth between them. With the forest of glass and steel spread out below me and the ground so far below, I know I should have felt fear, but all I felt was awe.

"It is beautiful," I whispered.

"It is indeed," a warm alto voice behind me agreed. "It is my favorite view."

"It is so peaceful here. My mother would like this."

The voice laughed softly.

"Your mother is a very wise woman."

Suddenly the light dimmed and the city scape below was eclipsed by the vast night sky above me. From this height the stars were clearer and brighter than I had ever seen them.

I reached out my hand certain the golden twinkling Cygnus was within my reach.

"I think I like this view even better," I said.

"The stars spread out across the universe is a wonder even to a Goddess."

"Are you really Athena?"

"Who else would I be?"

"But you cannot really be the Goddess Athena. This is just a dream."

"Surely a Goddess could visit her followers in their dreams."

"A Goddess can do anything."

"So perhaps I am the real Athena and not just part of your dream."

"But how would I know the difference?"

"Ask me a question that you do not know the answer for. See if I am real or just in your mind."

"How many stars are there in the universe?"

"Too many to count, Ardella. Try again."

"Did we really come to Arcadia from a planet orbiting one of those stars?"

"Earth. Olympians and mortals alike call that distant blue world home."

"Do you miss it?"

"What a strange question – a child's question. Arcadia is a perfect world designed by my own hand. Earth was never perfect."

"But you still miss it sometimes, don't you?"

Her soft laughter filled the night air.

"Yes, Ardella, I do miss Earth – sometimes."

Chapter 3

From the journal of Lyessa, princess of the Amazons

The 3rd day of the month of Athena
Two thousand six hundred and thirty years Ab Terra Condita

Copy of her letter to Queen Brianna of Amazonia

Dear Mother,

    I have arrived safely in New Athens and Lady Lucinda has helped me register for the Academy. Rather than dividing into cohorts, classes here are assigned by subject. I will be taking Life Science, Advanced Geometry, Ancient Earth History, Choral Music and Physical Education. It is still a few days until classes begin, so Ardella and her mother have been showing me around New Athens.

    We attended a lecture on marine mammals at the Lyceum. Almost a hundred people (adults and students) crowded in the lecture hall to watch the holographic depictions of dolphins, whales

and other Earth and Arcadian sea life. I
think my sister Amazons would be
shocked to know that attending lectures
and visiting museums is what most people
in New Athens do with their free time.

We also visited the Arcadian History
Archive. Stepping into the Exhibition Hall
was like stepping into another world. The
lights, sounds, and even smells changed as
we stepped through the glass doors and
seem to actually walk into the past. There
is nothing like it in Amazonia.

There is a wing for each Olympian
and their followers. It was so large that I
was only able to explore a small part of it.
I learned so many new things about the
followers of Poseidon and their
underwater city Atlantis and saw an
incredible miniature replica of the glass
pyramids of Heliopolis.   (I hope I get to
see the real ones someday.)

Ardella wanted to show me the
Amazon wing, but sadly we ran out of
time. She said it is not nearly
as good as really going to Amazonia. I
hope we get to come back again before I
must return home.

Thank you again for allowing me to attend the Academy. I am looking forward to my classes and I promise to make the most of this opportunity. I will do my very best to make you and my sisters proud. Please give my love to Anna and Serena.

Love your daughter,
 Lyessa

The 4th day of the month of Athena

Ardella and I were in the small garden this afternoon practicing with the Bodan staves, when Rafe joined us. I am not sure if he came out to watch us fight or just to annoy us. He is very good at being annoying.

"What's that?" Rafe asked, strolling up under the tree where Ardella and I sat resting from our exertions.

"It's called a Bodan staff. It is the weapon my fighting cohort is currently learning to use back in Amazonia," I replied without looking up at the source of the question.

"Lyessa is teaching me to fight," Ardella added.

I couldn't help but smile at the enthusiasm in her comment.

"Why would you need to learn that? There is no war on Arcadia. What's the point of learning to fight?"

I watched Ardella's face fall at her brother's mocking questions, and felt the heat of anger rising in my cheeks. It was one thing to annoy me; it was much worse to annoy one of my friends – even if the friend was his sister.

"Amazons learn to defend ourselves, and if it ever becomes necessary we can defend Amazonia," I replied, frowning as I looked up at Rafe's smug face.

"Besides physical training is an excellent way to keep our bodies fit."

"Just like we have to take physical education at the Academy," Ardella agreed.

"I guess swinging sticks around would seem like fighting to girls," Rafe muttered, looking at Ardella with a scowl.

"You haven't even tried it, Rafe. It's not as easy as it looks!" Ardella said defensively.

"If you can do it, Ardella, it can't be all that hard," Rafe scoffed.

"Rafe!" I called loudly, throwing my Bodan staff his direction as soon as he turned towards me.

I was surprised and a little disappointed when he reached up and caught the staff smoothly with one hand. (I had secretly hoped it would smack him in the face for his attitude toward Ardella, and I could pretend it was an accident.)

"What are you doing?" he snapped.

"A challenge!" I told him. "Fight with the Bodan staff or shut up and go away."

"Lyessa, he is not worth it," Ardella said.

"If my sister can fight with this Bodan staff, so can I," Rafe said, moving the staff in a wide arch in front of him.

"Then you should fight Ardella," I replied.

"I'm not sure that is a good idea," Ardella said softly.

"Yeah. I don't want to fight her. I want to fight an Amazon."

I ignored Rafe's comment and focused on my friend's hesitation. I knew she was ready to face a real opponent, even if she wasn't certain. Perhaps a chance to swing at her brother was just what she needed.

"Are you sure, Ardella? I believe you are ready."

"I don't think I could make myself hit Rafe – no matter how annoying he is."

"I can't imagine not wanting to hit him," I commented.

"Hey!" Rafe huffed, twirling the Bodan staff.

"If you will loan me your staff, Ardella, I guess I will have to conduct Rafe's lesson myself."

"Don't hurt him too badly," she laughed, as she threw her staff towards me.

"Very funny," Rafe replied, twirling the staff. He stared at me with an intensity in his gaze that reminded me a little of my sister Amazons. He wanted to win this fight. Perhaps boys weren't so different after all.

"I'm ready," he said.

I moved out into the open area of the yard and swung the Bodan staff into the traditional defensive stance. Rafe mimicked my actions and stood before me. I thought I saw a flash of doubt in his eyes, but it was quickly gone.

He had the courage of an Amazon. For a moment, I thought I wouldn't go too hard on him, but then I remembered his rudeness to his sister.

"You are in defensive position one. It is how we begin all fights, since it allows you to move or swing in any direction."

"Swing at me overhand, and I will show you how to deflect the blow."

"I don't want a lesson. I want to fight."

"You have no experience fighting with a Bodan staff. I would be taking advantage of you, if I allowed you to fight me without any instruction at all."

"I don't need any lessons to swing a stick. Let's begin."

"As you wish," I said with a sigh. "Although you must know the basic rules." I added.

"Whatever."

"If you disarm your opponent or trap them on the ground, it counts as a victory. Blows to the head are not allowed as they could cause serious injury."

"Got it."

"Since you are new to the Bodan staff, I will give you the first swing."

Rafe took a deep breath and leaned to his right. Anticipating that he would now swing up and to the left, I raised my Bodan staff above my head and stopped his swing just as it began.

I saw the look of surprise on his face, and tried to ignore the rush of satisfaction that flowed through me. Ardella's brother need to be taught a lesson, and it was not a lesson on how to use the Bodan staff.

He shuffled back and adjusted his staff. I watched as he prepared to swing again. This time his body language told me he would swing to the right. Again, I blocked the blow before he could finish the full swing.

For the next few minutes I let Rafe attempt different swings from different angles as he became familiar with the Bodan staff. I was impressed with his creativity and the consistent strength of his blows over time. I remember how heavy the Bodan staff became the first time I fought, but Rafe showed no signs of fatigue.

That didn't mean he had any hope of winning this battle. I had yet to even strike a blow. I decided I had given him enough time to practice attacking.

"Not bad," I told him. "Now it is time to see how well you can defend yourself."

That was all the warning he got before I began my attack. My first offensive blow was the same as the first swing he had taken at me. Although it took him longer to realize my intent than it had taken me, he managed to bring his Bodan staff up to block the blow just before it reached his right shoulder.

Being new to the Bodan staff, he hadn't bend his elbows to help absorb the blow, so the jolt of staff meeting staff sent him stumbling backwards trying to keep from falling. If a sister Amazon had made such a mistake, I would have used a quick second blow to finish off my opponent and leave them laying on the ground.

Instead I allow Rafe to regain his balance and once again take up the defensive stance.

"Bend your elbows and lean into the blow you are deflecting to keep me from knocking you backwards," I advised.

Instead of the goading me with one of his sarcastic comments, he simply nodded his head and waited for the next attack.

He was actually listening to my advice - that was progress.

For the next few minutes I became the aggressor in our match. I attacked again and again; varying my swings to force him to concentrate on defending himself. I never gave him the opportunity to think about attack. With his mind and body totally engaged in stopping my blows, I finally saw him begin to tire.

The next time he raised the Bodan staff to block me I pushed back from the impact and swung low – aiming for his leg. I heard his gasp of surprise (and possibly pain) as my staff hit the back of his calf with enough force to make him lose his balance.

This time I followed up with a straight blow to his chest that left him flat on his back and holding the Bodan staff with only one hand. That was all I needed. I kicked the staff; sending if flying from his weakened grip and placed the butt of my staff against his chest.

I had disarmed him and had him pinned to the ground. Anna would have been pleased I had learned her lessons so well.

"I win," I announced.

I could hear Ardella applauding my victory, but my eyes were locked with Rafe's. He looked up at me for a very long time not saying a word. His gaze no longer held anger or contempt, but the fierce glow of determination.

"Will you teach me to do that?" he asked in a serious tone, totally unlike his earlier mockery.

I forced myself not to smile as I moved the staff and offered my hand to help him up. I hoped I had won more than just the match, but there was still a doubt in the back of my mind. Considering his earlier attitude, I wondered if he would take my hand.

I should not have been worried. Rafe didn't hesitate to accept by assistance, and I pulled him up until our noses were almost touching. This time I allowed myself to smile.

"I will give you lessons in the Bodan staff under one condition," I told him.

I saw his familiar scowl return at my words.

"What do you want?"

"You have stop teasing your sister and her friends."

"That's stupid."

"That is the price for your Bodan staff lessons. Take it or leave it."

Chapter 4
From the diary of Ardella of New Athens

The 6th day of the month of Athena
Two thousand six hundred and thirty years Ab Terra Condita

Today we moved back into the dorms. Classes begin tomorrow.   I am too excited to sleep, so I am writing instead.

I still remember how nervous I was the first time Mother brought me to the Academy. *Was that really only six months ago?*   I actually begged her not to leave me, and she had to patiently remind me **again** that it was the will of the Goddess. Mother promised me it would be alright, and she was right.

This time I am happy to be at the Academy. The Headmaster approved Lyessa and I becoming roommates. Elana, my former roommate, was very understanding about the switch, although she made me promise I would keep tutoring her in history.

Just before she left, Mother gave me her copy of the book required for Mistress Rhianna's Ancient Earth History course. I couldn't believe she would trust me with such a treasure.

Of course, the gift left most of my friends confused. They wanted to know if it was it some sort of punishment?   (It is a little big.)

Jason Nethercut's ***Complete History of Ancient Earth*** is easily four times the size of any other textbook they had ever seen. I guess three thousand years of history is hard to condense into a single source. Most of the other students, including Lyessa, chose to download the immense tome onto their crystal readers to avoid lugging something that heavy back and forth to class, but I love it and will carry it proudly.

I took Lyessa on a tour of the campus and showed her where all her classes would be. I am happy she was able to get into Mistress Rhianna's history class with me, but still don't understand why the Headmaster placed her in the same Physical Education class as Rafe. She will be the only girl.

Lyessa only laughed at my concern and reminded me her placement in classes had been based upon skill level, not gender or age. Besides, she told me, even the male physical education class won't be as challenging as fighting practice in an Amazon training cohort.

We walked past Rafe and his friends playing Triad during the tour. I spotted Demetrius almost immediately. Normally I would have just hurried past and pretend I didn't see him or hear the rude comments he made about me under his breath, but Lyessa wanted to stay and watch the game.

I had never really stopped to watch a Triad game before. I knew there were three players on each side, hence the name Triad, and that it involved throwing a small leather ball around, but that was the extent of my knowledge.

As we watched, Lyessa explained that Rafe and his two team members must pass the ball back and forth without allowing the other team to intercept the ball. Scoring is based upon who has control of the ball when the timer sounds at random intervals.

Although the rules forbid physical contact between players and said a ball could only be intercepted when it is in midair, I couldn't help but notice how often the boys accidentally ran into each other while playing. Rafe was knocked to the ground three times in the short time we stopped to watch the game.

After Rafe and Demetrius' team won the game, they came over to where Lyessa and I stood watching. Demetrius stared a Lyessa for a long time before he stated the obvious in a manner that suggested he was annoyed.

"You're new."

"This is Lyessa," Rafe said in a much more cordial tone.

He actually sounded friendly.

Demetrius scoffed. "So, you're the Amazon Rafe won't stop talking about."

I saw Rafe's face redden, fortunately Demetrius didn't. He was still staring at Lyessa.

"You don't look so tough to me. All those stories about the Amazons must be lies."

I wanted to protest Demetrius' rude attitude toward my friend, but past experience had taught me acknowledging his words only encouraged him to continue. I turned to Lyessa planning to suggest she just ignore him.

It turns out my advice was unnecessary.

Lyessa didn't even look over Demetrius (which made him turn red) and instead directed her comment to my brother.

"Congratulations on your victory, Rafe. You're an excellent Triad player."

"Thanks," Rafe replied – again in a friendly, sincere tone, and he was still blushing.

What was going on? What had this imposter done with my annoying brother?

Of course, Demetrius couldn't stand being ignored.

"What would you know about Triad?" Demetrius asked in the bullying whine he often used when speaking to me.

Lyessa sighed – a full sound that made it clear she regretted having to speak to him, but he had given her no choice.

I laughed as our eyes met briefly and I could almost hear her thoughts *"Boys are so annoying!"*

"I only play Triad occasionally, but my older sisters are champions," she informed him.

"Girls don't play Triad," Demetrius announced pompously, as if he were some sort of expert on the subject. I realized with some satisfaction that he was the only one present who didn't know how wrong he was.

I rolled my eyes at him, and almost felt sorry for what was about to happen.

"Girls don't play Triad?" Lyessa crooned now fully focused on Demetrius. She moved slowly and deliberately toward him like a cat playing with a mouse and asked, "Who told you that?"

"I guess…" he stammered, stepping back instinctively.

Lyessa showed no mercy.

"You do know there are only girls in Amazonia, so if girls don't play Triad, how do I know that you earned at least three holding penalties that no one called you on."

"You don't know anything about how …" Demetrius blustered, but Lyessa continued as if he hadn't spoken.

"The rules of Triad state that if the same player keeps the ball in their possession without passing it for more than 15 seconds the opposing team may call a holding penalty. True?"

Suddenly Demetrius was silent.

"That's true, but the other team has to call the holding," Rafe confirmed.

"Then your opponents were being generous, since each holding penalty could have earned them a point. You only won by two points."

"Does that mean the other team should have won?" I asked.

"Technically," Lyessa replied.

"It was just a friendly game," Demetrius huffed. "We don't have to be so strict with the rules."

"Understandable, although my sister Amazons would never be so generous to an opponent."

"The other team didn't call the holding penalties on Demetrius because they're scared of him," Rafe announced with a laugh.

"Hey! Whose side are you on?" Demetrius bellowed.

"Yours, dummy. Why do you think I like playing Triad with you, Demetrius? Because of that fear, we always win."

"Rafe, that's cheating," I said.

"No, Ardella. It's doing what it takes to win."

"I don't cheat!" Demetrius whined.

Lyessa shook her head and laughed.

"Not on purpose," she said, looking straight at Rafe. "But that is not true for everyone on your team."

Why did Lyessa sound like she approved of my brother's method of winning?

"It's easy to watch Triad and count down the seconds, but it is very different when you are into the game. It is very fast-paced and challenging. You couldn't do it."

This time it was Rafe who rolled his eyes at Demetrius blunder.

"You play Triad in your Physical Education class, right?"

"Yeah. Are you going to come watch us play?"

"Not exactly."

"What does that mean?" Demetrius asked.

"It means she's was assigned to our PE class, dummy. The Headmaster said it was the only one that might come close to her Amazon training requirements," Rafe said.

Demetrius was actually speechless, but my brother wasn't.

"And next time we pick Triad teams, I think I am going to want to be on Lyessa's side. The other boys may fear you, but Lyessa plays to win."

The 7th day of the month of Athena

The first day back at school was wonderful, but it has been a very long day. I realize now that the teachers went easy on us last trimester, since we were new to the Academy. There had been games to help us learn the names of our classmates and activities to practice proper study techniques.

Looking back, actual lessons and homework assignments had not really begun the first few days. That was not true for my second trimester at the Academy. Even Mistress Rhianna gave us a reading assignment for homework. We were beginning our study of Ancient Earth History with the Greeks and the origins of human civilization. It was going to be interesting, but lots and lots of reading.

I am not so enthusiastic about my Writing class. Our first assignment is to write a personal narrative. I have no idea what to write about. Nothing interesting enough to write about ever happens to me. Lyessa laughed when I complained about the assignment.

"How many girls at the Academy have visited Amazonia?" she had asked.

When I look at it from Lyessa's perspective, maybe I do have something to write about.

My name is Ardella. My mother is a professor at the Academy who specializes in Ancient Earth History. Because of her great knowledge of Earth "pop" culture, the Queen of the Amazons invited her to come to Amazonia to analyze a **Wonder Woman** comic book recently discovered in their Archives.

My visit to Amazonia taught me that books cannot teach me everything there is to know about Arcadia. My geography class taught me that Lake Hera was the biggest body of fresh water

on Arcadia, but I never really understood
just how big Lake Hera was until I saw it
with my own eyes.

As we stood on the shore loading
the barge that would take us to Amazonia,
I could not see anything but water in front
of us. How could there be so much water
between us and the island? For a while
you could see nothing but water in every
direction. It made me feel small and
mortal, in a way that even standing in the
shadow of Athena's tower never had
before.

My second example is Amazonia
itself. When the island of Amazonia
finally came into review, it was nothing
like I expected. It was like a huge wild
park filled with so many trees and flowers
that they far outnumbered the buildings
and walking paths created by the mortals.
It didn't feel like a city, but a natural work
of art.

My last example of books not
teaching me as much as experience is my
friend Lyessa. The books my mother
gave me about Amazons told me about
their training and customs.

What I learned from Lyessa is that
Amazons are more than a list of rules or a
description of their culture. Lyessa is
dedicated. To her being an Amazon is
about pushing herself to learn and grow
into the best possible version of herself

she can be. She never stops training,
and everything she does is to make the
Queen of the Amazons and the Goddess
Hera proud.

The differences between books
and reality taught me a valuable lesson.
Places are more than just geography and
facts. Places are made up of many
different mortals who see our world
through the eyes of different Olympians.

Thanks to Lyessa's suggestion, I earned an A on my personal narrative.

One thing that I did not include in the assignment (because I was not sure how the teacher would react) was how much I learned about the nature of mortals during my trip.

I learned that no matter which Olympian we follow, we all have basic human needs, fears, joys and dreams. Mortals are more alike than the Olympians would have us believe. That is why I can have so much in common with my friend Lyessa even though she follows Hera and I follow Athena.

Chapter 5

<u>From the journal of Lyessa, princess of the Amazons</u>

The 12th day of the month of Athena

Two thousand six hundred and thirty years Ab Terra Condita

Copy of her letter to Princess Anna of Amazonia

Dear Anna,

The Academy is so different than our training cohorts back in Amazonia. Did you know that every class takes place inside buildings – even physical education? I do love learning new things, but being trapped inside all day makes me a little restless.

I can hear you laughing at me and pointing out how much time I spent in Mother's library at home, but remember my favorite chair (I miss it) overlooks the gardens and I may come and go as I please. At the Academy I must sit at tables in windowless rooms for hours at a time. It is harder than it sounds.

More than once I have found myself so stir crazy that I wanted to ask the teacher to excuse me for just a few minutes to walk around outside. Then I remembered Mother's warning that there can be no special treatment for an Amazon princess – I suppose that is especially true at the Academy.

Yesterday I decided to take my lunch from the dining hall and eat out under the grove of trees near the building just to spend a few minutes outside. Ardella followed me, because she was worried, and then stayed because she didn't want me to eat alone.   She is very sweet.

Today several other students followed Ardella and I out of the dining hall – curious about what we were doing.   In the end they all sat down and ate their lunch under the trees. They said they enjoyed eating outdoors and promised to join us again.

Even with the strangeness of being inside all day, I am pleased to say I am adjusting well in my classes – except perhaps physical education. All of the other students in the class are boys who seem to think my presence in "their" PE class is a problem.

I don't understand the issue. We
were all placed in the class because we
have similar skills and levels of physical
fitness, yet many of the boys are upset
that a girl might be as good an athlete
as they are. Ardella warned me this
would happen even before I started
the class. She tried to explain the
rivalry between boys and girls, but I am
afraid I will never understand.

Strangely enough the presence
of boys in my choral music class has a
harmonizing effect (no pun intended).
Don't get me wrong – I love singing
with my sister Amazons, but I never
realized something was missing until I
heard male voices fill out the
harmonies. Songs have a richer, fuller
sound when tenors and basses join the
altos and sopranos to sing.

Please give my love to Mother
and Serena.   I miss you all, but I
promise to make the most of this
opportunity at the Academy.

Love your sister,
  Lyessa

14th day of the month of Athena

Naniwa-zu ni-Sakuya kono haana/Fuyu-gomori, Ima o haru-be to-Sakuya kono hana

"Do you recognize the song?" Mistress Rhianna asked the class after the music from her crystal reader ended.

"The melody sounds like a song my mother sang to me when I was little," Tera suggested.

"Me, too, except those weren't the words I knew," Ardella added.

"Were they even words or just made up sounds?" Tera asked.

"They sounded like words, but I didn't know the meaning of a single one," Ardella said.

"What do you think Lyessa?" Mistress Rhianna asked.

"I didn't recognize the melody or the words. At first I thought it was because I was from Amazonia and didn't sing the same songs everyone else did as small children, but since no one seemed to understand the words, it must be something unusual from ancient Earth," I suggested.

"Excellent observation, Lyessa," Mistress Rhianna said. "The song is called ***Now the Flower Blooms***. It is from an island kingdom called Japan."

"But why can't we understand the words?" Ardella asked.

"Because the people in Japan did not speak the common language we do here on Arcadia. On ancient Earth, there was more than one way to communicate – more than one language."

"More than one language? Why would the Olympians create more than one language?" Tera asked.

"They didn't. Language is not a gift of the Olympians. It is part of being mortal. During the dark times on Earth the Olympians lost control over mankind and as a result many different languages developed."

"Mortals on Earth created languages?" a student in the back asked in hushed voice of awe.

"Mortals can be very creative. In many ways mankind's imagination is superior to the Olympians," Mistress Rhianna said.

There was a long silence.   Although I had seen more open-minded teaching methods since my arrival at the Academy, I realized even the free-thinking children of Athena were dumbfounded to have a teacher suggesting mortals were better than Olympians at anything.

Mistress Rhianna ignored the gasp of shock and surprise that washed over her small classroom, and continued the lesson.

"Unfortunately, different languages made communication among mortals difficult and contributed to the violence and fighting that drove us from Earth. That is why the Olympians have all mortals speak a common language on Arcadia. It is meant to promote peace and harmony."

"Like the Great Law of the Olympians," Ardella said.

"Very good," Mistress Rhianna said.

"What does the song say – in our language?" Ardella asked.

"In Naniwa Bay, now the flowers are blossoming. After lying dormant all winter, now the spring has come and those flowers are blossoming," Mistress Rhianna replied.

"Those are silly words," Demetrius grumbled.

"It's a song celebrating the return of Spring," I suggested.

"It sounded better in Japanese," Demetrius said.

The class laughed.

We went on to spend the rest of the time discussing Ares' influence on a warrior class in Japan called the Samurai. Despite being fascinated by the stories and pictures of these swordsmen, I still had one more question about languages on ancient Earth.

As the rest of the class departed, I approached the teacher's desk and asked, "Mistress Rhianna, did any of the languages from ancient Earth make it to Arcadia?"

"Only one - a language used by the ancient Romans called Latin."

"Can we learn Latin?" I heard Ardella ask from behind me.

No surprise that my best friend had remained behind with me to learn more about ancient Earth.

"Probably not. It is a language reserved for only a select few at Academy and the members of the Council of Athena. No one else may know it."

"Why?" Ardella asked.

Although Ardella's question was simple and direct, I suspected the answer to her inquiry would be Olympian in nature.

"To keep secrets," I speculated.

“Exactly. Knowledge is power,” Mistress Rhianna confirmed. “No one knows that better than the Goddess Athena.”

Chapter 6
From the diary of Ardella of New Athens

The 15th day of the month of Athena
Two thousand six hundred and thirty years Ab Terra Condita

My friend Lyessa is restless. She is not used to spending so much time indoors. The other day she actually took her lunch outside the cafeteria and sat down to eat on the grass. She convinced me a picnic was just the break we needed from our classes. She was right. It was nice.

I would never have dared such a thing on my own, but she made it sound fun. She has encouraged me to try many new things since I met her. Unfortunately, she has had a similar effect on Rafe. This is the third evening in a row that she has gone out to the quad to practice the Bodan staff with my brother.

I guess I should be happy my twin is no longer being rude to my best friend. *Who would have known that knocking him to the ground with a Bodan staff was the best way to get him to stop being so annoying?* He is even being nicer to me to get Lyessa to give him Bodan staff lessons.

I am not sure why, but I don't feel happy about the strange twist in our lives.

I know Rafe and Lyessa have a lot in common. They are both adventurous and athletic. They even seem to have a similar sense of humor.

I am beginning to think they have more in common than Lyessa and I do. We both love books, but my best friend is good at so many other things.

I am afraid she will get bored with me.

I ran into Mother today outside Mistress Rhianna's Ancient Earth class. (She just happened to be passing by as the class let out.) She wanted to know how I was liking Ancient Earth History. When she asked who my favorite historical figure was, I told her there were too many fascinating Earth mortals to choose from.

Of course, my brain would not let the question go, and has been thinking about it all day – which has interfered greatly with the homework I was supposed to be doing.

After weighing all the options, I have narrowed it down to three favorites.

One is Alexander the Great. He was a young Macedonian prince who happened to be a Son of Ares. What I found fascinating about him is that he was trained in Athens by a follower of Athena named Aristotle. He learned both the art of war and leadership from the Goddess of Wisdom, and then his father's nature drove him to conquered many lands and created a great empire that lived on even after his death.

The second is an Egyptian queen named Cleopatra. She was only fourteen years old when she found herself in a civil war with her brother Ptolemy, and there was the interference of an older, powerful Roman named Caesar.

She was a Daughter of Hera (who the Egyptians called Isis) and managed to turn the situation to her advantage. She formed an alliance with Caesar and defeated her brother to become the ruler of Egypt.

My final choice is a Roman emperor named Vespasian. He was a common soldier with no ties to any Olympian. He rose through the ranks of the Roman army on his own merit to become a powerful Legionary Commander. After the death of Nero (one of the more embarrassing Sons of Dionysus), he seized control of the Roman Empire and became popular with the people for his wise and stable rule. Most of the great leaders on ancient Earth we study have Olympian parents, but it is nice to know that there were at least a few important mortals, too.

We are almost finished with the Classical period. The next part of the book is on the Age of Chivalry and the Renaissance. It is the beginning of the Dark Ages on Earth where the Olympians started losing control of mankind – not that they didn't continue to meddle in human affairs.

The 17th day of the month of Athena

I was rushing to meet Lyessa behind the library for our Ancient Earth study session. I had let my best friend convince me that reading beneath the shade of the giant oak trees would make learning more fun. I suspected Lysi was just looking for an excuse to spend more time outdoors, but I was willing to play along to make my friend happy.

I knew Lyessa had beaten me to the meeting spot even before I rounded the corner of the library, when I heard her voice loud and clear.

"I don't think that's a good idea!"

"You're not afraid, are you?" Ardella heard the familiar voice of her brother Rafe ask.

I stopped abruptly. *What was he doing here?*

"Why would I be afraid? I have been face-to-face with silver lupines on Mt. Orion and there weren't behind the bars of a cage."

"Then you will come with me to the Menagerie? I have watched Father open the doors many times. I can get us in to see it."

"If you want to see what **Genotec** has created so badly, why don't you just ask your Father's permission?"

My mind raced at the word **Genotec**. Where had I heard that name before?

"What's the fun in that?" Rafe laughed.

He sounded cocky and up to no good. That was the twin brother I was used to.

"I am sure I could get Father to tell me what mythical monster the athletes will have to face," he boasted. "The challenge of seeing it for myself without getting caught is the fun part."

Suddenly it came to me. **Genotec** was the genetic engineering branch of the Academy that created real life mythical monsters like Chimeras and Manticores for the Olympic Games. Last year's Cerberus had made me nervous around dogs for months.

"Rafe, you are reckless to take such risks when you don't have to," Lyessa advised, and I felt myself nodding in approval at her wise words.

Rafe was not convinced.

"I can't help it!" he protested. "It's in my nature. I crave more than I can learn from dusty books encircled by the stone walls of Athena's *perfect* Academy. I need to do something – to take risks."

"That's not very Athenian of you."

"I am not a perfect Athenian like Ardella and my parents. I don't always fit in here. Sometimes I just feel trapped and …"

"Need to break the rules," Lyessa said with just hint of admiration in her voice.

I had heard enough. It was time to make my presence known before my mischievous brother talked my best friend into doing something rash.

"I thought you might understand," I heard Rafe mutter, as I forced herself back into motion and rounded the corner of the library.

"Good afternoon, Lyessa," I said cheerfully.

Rafe looked over at me with a mixture of guilt and suspicion. His questioning stare meant he was wondering how much I had overheard. I just smiled.

"Good afternoon, Rafe."

Chapter 7

<u>From the journal of Lyessa, princess of the Amazons</u>

The 18th day of the month of Athena

Two thousand six hundred and thirty years Ab Terra Condita

Mistress Rhianna's announcement that we would be straying from today's planned lesson on Chivalry to meet a visiting Olympic athlete was met with spontaneous applause from everyone in the class, except maybe Ardella. I was not surprised. My best friend had gotten quiet and moody every time someone had mentioned the Olympic Games lately.

Talk about the games seemed to happen more and more often, since the Olympics were due to begin in a few weeks at the sporting complex just outside New Athens. The entire Academy would be on vacation for the duration of the games, so everyone could attend.

Since the Olympic Games were always held in New Athens, I had never had the chance to see them before. I was especially excited to get to watch this year's Olympics, since my sisters were part of the Amazon team.

"While we are waiting for our visiting Olympic athlete to arrive, let's see what you remember about the Ancient Earth Olympics," Mistress Rhianna announced.

Demetrius' groan of protest brought a round of laughter from the class. It also focused Mistress Rhianna attention squarely on the class bully. He was about to pay for his outburst, and I had no sympathy.

"Thank you for volunteering to go first, Demetrius," she said with a sickly-sweet tone that sent a shiver up my spine and almost made me feel sorry for him. Almost.   "Tell us one thing you know about the ancient Earth Olympics."

His brow crinkled in concentration as he searched his mind for an acceptable answer. Suddenly his eyes lit up and he smiled.

"Only men were allowed to participate," he said, looking over at me.

His smirk told me that he hoped I would take offense. He really didn't understand Amazons. I had better things to do than worry about Demetrius's feeble attempts to annoy me.

"And they competed naked," another student added.

This answer drew laughter from many of the students in the class.

"That is true. The Greeks of ancient Earth were fascinated by the perfection of the human body. That is why most of their statues were nude as well."

Again, the class giggled, and I found myself rolling my eyes at their childishness. That drew Mistress Rhianna's eyes to me.

"What else do you know about the ancient Olympics? Lyessa?"

"Throwing the discus and javelin were two of the contests in the Olympics – just like today," I replied.

"Very good," Mistress Rhianna said, and then began looking around at the class expectantly. I could not help but notice the keen appraisal she gave each student reminded me of the scrutiny of silver lupine searching for its next meal.

"Who were the ancient Olympics in honor of, Tera?" Mistress Rhianna asked.

There was silence.

"Athena?" she asked rather than answered.

"Not Athena. Ardella, do you know?"

"The Olympics were established by Heracles, a Son of Zeus, who held them in his father's honor," Ardella replied.

"That is correct. The first Olympic Games were in honor of Zeus and included a stade race, a ..."

"The Olympics are in honor of Zeus?" Demetrius interrupted loudly. "That doesn't make any sense. Wasn't he Olympian that..."

Demetrius' question came to an abrupt halt when all eyes in the class fixed on him. I saw him gulp hard as if trying to swallow whatever he had been about to say. I could see the fear creeping into his eyes. This time I did feel a little sorry for him, since Mistress Rhianna was intolerant of such outbursts in class.

"Although that was the wrong way to ask his question, Demetrius has brought up an important point that we should discuss. Why were the ancient Olympics in honor of Zeus?"

The hush that engulfed the classroom was uncomfortable. The question Mistress Rhianna had asked was impossible to answer. Zeus was not a name that was mentioned very often at the Academy or anywhere on Arcadia. Looking around at the other puzzled faces in class, I realized I was not alone in my ignorance.

"Zeus was a powerful Olympian. On ancient Earth he was the God of the Sky and leader of the Olympians who opposed Mother Hestia," Mistress Rhianna said. "He was also the husband of the Goddess Hera."

All eyes now turned my direction.

"I would be curious to know what the followers of Hera are told about Zeus." Mistress Rhianna said.

Her curious gaze told me that this wasn't a traditional Academy question with a right or wrong answer. My teacher was requesting information that I had, and she did not. I'm not sure that had ever happened to me before. I found myself wanting to impress her with my reply.

"The Amazons learn that Zeus was not a very good husband to Hera nor a very good ruler over those who followed him. Fed up with his many faults, Hera changed sides. She joined Mother Hestia in the civil war between the Olympians and help defeat her husband."

"What happened to Zeus?" Tera asked me and not Mistress Rhianna.

I hesitated, looking up at our history teacher who only smiled and nodded for me to continue.

"Hera insisted he be abandoned on Earth when all the other Olympians left for Arcadia, so she would never have to deal with him again."

"Hera left behind an Olympian husband on Earth! No wonder mortal men aren't allowed in Amazonia," Demetrius commented and again the class erupted into laughter.

To my surprise, Demetrius flushed obviously embarrassed and for a moment I thought he was going to apologize for his thoughtless words. *That would have been a first.*

Unfortunately, the guest Olympian athlete (a javelin thrower from the followers of Apollo in Heliopolis) chose that moment to arrive, and all questions about Zeus and the ancient Olympics were forgotten in the excitement.

The 19th day of the month of Athena

I would prefer to pretend that the story I am about to tell did not really happen, but I am recording the tale of my unfortunate choices and the dangerous consequences to remind myself NEVER to do something so reckless again. ***May Hera forgive me, if Mother every finds out!***

A cold shiver crept up my spine as I waited in the shadow of one of the ancient oak trees behind the library. I didn't think it was the midnight air that made me shiver, but the reason I was out here that chilled my bones.

For the first time in my life I was doing something stupid and against the rules. It wasn't at all like me, and yet I found the act of defiance thrilling – just like Rafe said I would. *Ardella's brother managed to be annoying, even when he wasn't present.*

I had waited until everyone was asleep to sneak out of the dormitory. I was waiting exactly where Rafe and I had agreed to meet. It was just taking him longer to get here, and unfortunately, I was left with nothing to do but wait. That gave me far too much time to think about what I was planning to do.

This idea was crazy. Why would I risk my future at the Academy to see some mythical monster trapped within the confines of a cage? It was stupid. I didn't need to preview the monster **Genotec** created for the Olympic Games. I would see it soon enough in the arena.

So why had I let Rafe talk me into this?   That was a good question.

Just as I had almost convinced myself that Rafe wasn't coming and returning to the dorms was the smartest thing I could do; my senses went on full alert. Someone was coming. Instincts perfected during my survival training on Mt. Orion took control.

My body was motionless against the dark trunk of the tree. I had worn my hunting cloak and knew that unless I did something to draw attention to myself, most people would walk right past me without even realizing I was there.

Opening up my other senses I waited for a sound, sight or smell that would tell me who else was out for a nocturnal stroll. My heart raced as I struggled to determine who else was there. Was it Rafe? Was it one of the Guardians?

I saw a flash of moonlight off to my right. Turning my head just slightly I caught sight of shadowy figure moving among the trees on the far side of the library. Observing for a few moments, I realized the figure was pacing between two trees.

That had to be Rafe – *impatient as ever*.

I made my way towards him moving quickly from one tree to the next. I made sure I only moved when he was faced away from me - just as I had been taught. Deianera, my survival trainer, would be proud of me. I successfully remained hidden within the dark shadows of the ancient trees.

In fact, it became a game – how close could I get before Rafe noticed me?

As I stood motionless only two trees away, I could see the worried expression on his face and could almost feel the nervous energy as he paced. I admit I was a little disappointed. Rafe had not sensed my presence nor did he even suspect I stood near. I suppose he was at a disadvantage because he had not been through survival training like I had.

"Where is she?" I heard him mutter, and I had to stop myself from giggling.

I was so close and he didn't have a clue.

"She's not coming. She changed her mind. Wait! What if she got caught sneaking out? If I talked her into doing something that gets her suspended from the Academy, Ardella is going to kill me," he mumbled, as he paced.

I couldn't stay silent any longer.

"If I were a silver lupine, you would be dinner by now," I said softly.

Rafe jerked to a stop and turned toward my voice. The fear was clear on his face. As his eyes met mine, however, the frightened expression turned to irritation.

"Why did you sneak up on me like that?"

"I was just practicing. I want to see how close I could get before you notice me."

"Practicing what?"

"Some of the survival skills I learned on Mt. Orion."

"Amazons learn survival skills?"

"Of course."

"Why?"

"It's part of our training. All Amazons must spend six weeks in the wilderness of Mt. Orion learning how to hunt for food, build fires, make shelters, and of course how to avoid wild animals such as bears and silver lupines."

"That sounds exciting. Much better than all the stupid stuff we have to learn at the Academy."

"It is not always fun, and six weeks is a long time. After so much time on Mt. Orion, I couldn't wait to get back to Mother's library."

"Really? You missed your books? I almost forgot you were one of Ardella's silly friends."

I smacked his arm.

"Ouch!"

"You promised not to tease."

"I promised not to tease Ardella. You never said I couldn't tease you."

"You promised not to tease any of Ardella's friends. I am one of Ardella's friends," I reminded him.

"Maybe, but…"

I smacked him again.

"Hey, stop that! Do you want to see the monster or not?"

"You are really so set on being the first to see the mythical monster for the Olympic Games that you are willing to risk getting caught sneaking into the Menagerie?"

"It will be exciting. We will be the only two students at the Academy who will know what is coming. Everyone else on Arcadia will have to wait and be surprised at the unveiling next month."

"Why is it so important to know?"

"Athena teaches that knowledge is power."

"I don't think that this is what she had in mind."

"I'm doing this. Are you coming or not?"

Despite my protests, I was curious, so I followed Rafe across campus to the large oval building that housed the Academy's Menagerie. I was surprised that we only encountered one Guardian that we had to avoid along the way. We would never have been able to sneak around like this in Amazonia.

As promised Rafe got us into the building without incident. He entered his father's code on the keypad, and the service door of the Menagerie magically opened.   I could not help but think that New Athens' dependence on electronic locks and passcodes was a weakness. We did not use such things in Amazonia. We had more guardians. Codes didn't protect things as well as people could.

Only moments after entering the Menagerie and closing the door behind us, Rafe startled me. Without warning he stopped dead in his tracks – causing me to bump into him in the dimly lit corridor.

"What's wrong?" I whispered. "Why did you stop?"

"Nothing's wrong. It's just…"

"What?"

"It's too quiet. I've never been here at night. During the day, the animals make lots of noise."

"Rafe!" I scolded, once again hitting his arm to express my displeasure.

"Hey, why do you keep hitting me?" he protested.

"Because you're annoying!" I snapped, although I honestly wondered myself why my first instinct was to hit him every time he decided to torment me with his teasing.

Maybe I was just off balance since my Amazon sisters never treated me this way.

"Which way to this mythical monster of yours?" I asked.

"It should be in the lower level where they keep the more dangerous creatures."

"Dangerous creatures? What dangerous things does this Menagerie hold?"

"The Menagerie holds at least one example of every animal on Arcadia. There are wild red bears from the Forest of Hestia, lions and shadow cats from the Great Savannah and even silver lupines from Mt. Orion."

"I doubt the silver lupines like living in a cage."

"We don't use cages. We provide natural habitats."

"I don't understand."

"Here. Let me show you," Rafe said, as he as he grabbed my hand and began pulling me down the dark corridor. I was too startled by his action to do anything but follow. As we moved through the stillness, however, I began to realize how strange it felt to be holding his hand.

"Here it is," he said, suddenly coming to a stop and dropping my hand to active a panel on the wall.

I looked over at him twice to be certain, but it was fairly obvious Rafe hadn't noticed the sensation that had passed between had caused me to blush. *Thank the Goddess!*

"Put your hand on the panel," Rafe instructed.

"What?" I murmured still a little flustered.

"The panel opens the habitat. You have to put your hand on it to enter," he replied, in a voice that was far more patronizing than I would have normally tolerated, but considering the circumstances, it seemed rude to protest.

I took a deep breath to calm my nerves and placed my hand on the panel. I immediately found myself in the cool night air of a temperate forest. This didn't alarm me, since I had been in the fighting arena in Amazonia often enough to recognize a simulation. The grove of Ash and Brentwood trees were familiar to me, but only from the images I had seen on my crystal reader.

"Is this the Forest of Hestia?" I whispered, looking up into the starry sky above us.

"I think so. It's the habitat of the horned owls. They are one of my favorite birds.

"I would expect nothing less of a follower of Athena."

"Look over there," he said, pointing a shadowy lump perched on the lower branch of a nearby tree.

Making a strange chirping noise, Rafe held his left arm straight out. The lump suddenly developed large yellow eyes and long feathery wings. Without making any sound or giving any advance warning, it took to the air. I gasped as I felt the vibration of the bird's powerful wings stir the hair near my right ear. It flew straight at Rafe and the arm that was doing a reasonably good tree limb imitation and landed with a graceful plop.

"Her name is Bebe," Rafe said, rubbing the crest on the top of its head with his free hand. There was a gentleness in his voice I wasn't accustomed to hearing.

"This is her habitat."

"This is much better than a cage," I agreed.

"There are no cages in New Athens."

"Does every creature in the Menagerie have its own habitat?"

"Pretty much. A few animals with strong symbiotic relationships share a common habitat."

"And the keepers can enter the simulation by touching the panel."

"Exactly. As soon as you let go of the panel you will be back in the corridor."

"Show me more!"

Rafe grinned, sent Bebe back to her original branch with the tilt of his arm, and then promptly disappeared. It took several attempts to instruct my own brain to move the hand in the corridor that I could not see rather than the one my eyes were certain they could see, but I finally managed to let go of the panel and join Rafe in the hall.

"I know at first it's hard to tell if you are moving your real body or the simulated one. It gets easier."

"Good to know."

"Do you want to see a shadow cat?"

"I would love to," I replied.

As I followed Rafe, I found myself thinking about what I had recently read about the conflict between the Amazons and the followers of Artemis.

"I read that the Goddess Artemis was away hunting a rare shadow cat when her followers were wiped out a thousand years ago."

"I'd never heard that."

"Artemis was a great huntress."

"That may be true, but that didn't help her followers."

"What do you mean?"

"I wonder what would have happened if the Goddess Artemis had been on the battlefield rather than out hunting? Do you think she could have saved her followers from their fate?"

"It wouldn't have made a difference. There was no stopping it."

"You don't believe we make our own destiny?"

I thought about my older sisters and peril the Fates had placed over their head since the day they were born. They didn't even know about the danger, yet it controlled their lives.

Even as Queen of the Amazons my mother could not escape the Fates. She was the most honored of all the Amazons and yet could not control destiny. A shiver crept up my spine as I thought of the terrible struggle she faced because of a thousand-year-old law and her duty to Hera.

"Between the power of the Olympians and the pull of the Fates, we mortals have little opportunity to control our own destiny."

"I don't plan to let the Fates or any Olympian control my life. Mortals have free will and I am going to use mine."

I could not help but admire the conviction of his words. I wished in that moment that I could believe that mortals had free will, but Amazon duty had taught me otherwise.

"Good luck with that," I muttered and then immediately regretted it.

What right did I have to belittle his dream? Just because Hera didn't allow her Amazons to choose for themselves didn't mean Athena might not be more tolerant.   Just as I opened my mouth to apologize, we arrived at our destination.

"Here is it," Rafe said, smiling at me.

I guess he either didn't hear my comment or didn't take offense at my doubts about free will. I sighed with relief and placed my hand on the panel.

This time I was standing in the tall grass of the Great Savannah. The warm night air blew across the slender golden blades causing them dance and sway. I reached down to run my hand along the bushy tips of the grass and felt it tickle my fingers. This was an excellent simulation.

"Hey wait for me!" Rafe grumbled a little too loudly as he suddenly appeared beside me on the savannah.

"Shh," I told him. "Shadow cats are night hunters. If you make too much noise, you will draw them right to us."

"That seems like a good way to find them."

"I want to see one up close, but it will be a very brief glimpse, if we are their prey."

"They can't really hurt us, Lyessa. This is just a simulation."

"I would think having your throat ripped out by a shadow cat would be as least as painful as having a harpy's claw enter your heart. I have not experienced it yet, but my sisters tell me the sensation is very painful."

"In Amazonia, your real body feels pain from what happens inside the simulation. I didn't know that was possible."

"The fighting arena is part of our Amazon training. It would give us a false sense of invulnerability, if we felt no pain in combat."

"That part of Amazon training doesn't sound so fun."

"Are you certain there is no pain feedback in the Menagerie's simulations? They did have the same Olympian designer after all."

"Just because Hephaestus designed both systems doesn't mean they work the same way," Rafe said, his voice just a little shaky. "But just in case, let's do this your way."

I smiled. When I first arrived in New Athens Ardella's brother had been rude and hostile. He had disliked me without even knowing me – just for being an Amazon.

But not anymore.

Even the Fates could not have foreseen this day. There was a boy from New Athens and a girl from Amazonia who had found common ground and despite their differences had become friends. Perhaps there was something to this idea of free will after all.

"Stand perfectly still and watch the grass for unusual movement. That will be the shadow cat," I whispered.

"But the wind is making the grass sway back and forth. How do you tell a shadow cat from the wind?" he replied in a hushed tone

"Look for movement that is opposite or different."

"Like that?" he asked pointing to a patch of grass bending against the wind.

"Exactly. Now we watch and wait."

Chapter 8
From the journal of Lyessa, princess of the Amazons

The 20th day of the month of Athena
Two thousand six hundred and thirty years Ab Terra Condita

I didn't get to finish my journal entry yesterday, because Ardella came back to our room wanting to study for today's Ancient Earth History Quiz. Thanks to her I earned a perfect score on the test.

My friend Ardella has a very scholarly mind. She naturally organizes information into small categories and creates tricks to help memorize the data more easily. (I am beginning to think she makes the study tools primarily for me, since she seems to have the ability to remember almost anything she reads without much difficulty.)

Whatever the reason, I am going to take her study method back with me to Amazonia. Mistress Rhea and my sisters Amazons in my cohort should be very impressed.

Ardella says her study aide is an ancient Earth technique called a mnemonic. It is a way to remember a list of words or phrases you wish to recall. You put them in order so that the first letter of each item forms a word. Then you use the word to help recall the list. I agree it is very useful.

Ardella made up a mnemonic for remembering the four Roman emperors who were Sons of Ares.

TiTAN (Tiberius, Trajan, Augustus and Nerva)

She also knew one for Biology that formed a sentence rather than a word.

King Proteus came over from Greek shores.

This one helps you remember the groupings of classification in taxonomy from largest to smallest: Kingdom, Phylum, Class, Order, Family, Genus, and Species.

I'm not sure if I am as truly fascinated by mnemonics as this entry would suggest, or if I am simply trying to avoid finishing yesterday's story.

Rereading my journal entry, it is clear I made many poor decisions that night, but I am still reluctant to describe how that chain of events lead up what could have been a great tragedy.

It is the stupidest thing I have ever done, and I still can't explain why I did it. I guess I was having too much fun to recognize the danger.

Mistress Rhea says we must never forget our mistakes. That helps us avoid them in the future. I suppose that means there is no more time for stalling.

Here is what happened next.

We stood there unmoving for a very long time watching the strange wave travel back and forth over the surface of the grass. I was fascinated knowing the surge was caused by the movement of a shadow cat below it, but it didn't take Rafe too long to get restless.

"It's not doing anything. Are you sure we are not just watching the wind move the grass around?" Rafe whispered.

"Shadow cats are one of the greatest hunters on all of Arcadia. They can remain hidden stalking their prey for hours."

"Hours?"

"They have great patience - unlike some people I know."

"Very funny. So how do we get it to hunt?"

Although I had a great deal more patience than Ardella's brother, I was beginning to suspect waiting was not the answer. After all – why would the simulation include creatures to hunt when the shadow cat would only be disappointed and confused when it finally made its kill?

No wonder it was pacing. *It must be bored out of its mind.*

"I suppose we will have to use your method after all."

"My method?"

I took one step forward and yelled, "SHADOW CAT, WHERE ARE YOU?"

For a moment Rafe looked horrified and then he laughed.

"I guess a brief glimpse is better than nothing," he commented, but quickly added, "But I'm letting go of the panel before it tears my throat out."

This time I laughed.

"You go that way," I said, pointing to the left. "I'll head toward where it was pacing earlier."

"Was pacing?" he said, looking quickly over at the grassy patch we had been staring at forever. There was no more wave. "It's gone. Where do you think it went?"

"I have no idea."

"So how do we find it again?"

"Start walking and it will find you."

I saw the flash of fear in his eyes and knew a similar emotion currently occupied mine as well. But Rafe wasn't going to let that stop him. He had the kind of courage to overcome his fears – just like an Amazon.

He grinned at me and then turned to walk in the direction I had suggested.

"Here, kitty, kitty," he called as he walked.

As I began walking, too, I cleared my mind and tried to concentrate on what my senses could tell me. I searched the waving grass for any signs of movement that might show where the shadow cat had gone. I strained to hear even the slightest sound, but Rafe's silly cries and the blood pounding in my ears made that endeavor useless.

"Use all your senses to track your prey. Open your mind and you will be amazed at what you can do," I heard Deianera's voice instructing me from a long-forgotten memory. Although survival skills had not been my favorite part of Amazon training, I was very grateful at this moment for all I had learned.

I could feel the soft grass tickle legs as I walked. I could smell the acrid tang of fear in the air. Was that me, or Rafe, or perhaps the shadow cat nervous about strangers in its habitat. The breeze blew across my flesh causing ripples of goose bumps. In fact, my whole body began to hum with anticipation. It was like skin could sense the approach of the elusive cat, even if my eyes and ears had failed.

Despite my Amazon training, terror began to grow within my heart. I had to make myself keep walking – one foot in front of the other – despite the panicked voice in my head that demanded I let go of the panel and get out of here **now**! My hands started to shake and my breath began to come harder and faster as if I had run a great distance

Just when I thought my fears might get the best of me, I saw them. Two iridescent purple eyes staring back at me from the hazy depths of the golden sea of grass directly in front of me. I froze as I struggled make out the rest of the shadow cat in the darkness.

As the cat's graceful face emerged from the night, my breath caught in my throat. Strangely enough it was not fear, but feline beauty that took my breath away. The shadow cat's long slender face was sleek and black - graced by two puffy tuffs that I could only assume were its ears.

The deep purple eyes that looked into mine were more curious than hostile. I felt my fear melt away as I realized the shadow cat had no plans to attack me. It was just curious and maybe a little lonely.

"Lyessa, I don't think there is a stupid shadow cat in this enclosure," Rafe called.

I rolled my eyes. The shadow cat let out a low hiss, as it turned towards the sound. It may not understand the words, but I was fairly certain it was more annoyed with the other intruder in its enclosure than I was at that moment.

Looking back at me, its expression was almost human and seemed to say, *Let me take care of the annoying thing first and then I'll be back.*

I watch fascinated as the dark panther burst forth from the shadows and bound toward Rafe. It was the most graceful creature I had ever seen. It was also headed straight for Rafe's throat.

"Look out, Rafe! It's headed your way."

I saw Rafe turn and heard his startled cry, "By the Goddess!"

Then he was gone, but the shadow cat was already in the air. Its long, sleek body flew in a graceful arch only to land with an awkward flop in the suddenly empty space.

Its hiss of displeasure and confusion filled the night, prompting my sympathy for the poor creature.

"Sorry kitty, he was never really here."

The shadow cat looked up with confused purple eyes at the sound of my voice. Even though it could not understand my words, it seemed to accept my sympathy.

"Just like I was never really here either," I added, then closed my eyes and let go of the panel.

It took a moment for my eyes to readjust to the light of the corridor. I was shocked and a little worried to find Rafe doubled up on the floor. The sounds coming from him made it clear he was having trouble breathing. *What could possibly be wrong? Did the shadow cat manage to hurt him somehow?*

I bent down to examine him and discovered the strange sounds were peals of laughter. In fact, he was laughing so hard that his face had turned red.

"What is wrong with you?" I hissed, slapping his arm, annoyed to have once again be frightened by his odd behavior.

"That… was…unbelievable," he managed to reply between gulps of air. "I saw… the look in its eyes. It was going … to eat me."

I shook my head.

"I doubt it. She wasn't hungry, just annoyed that you were in her enclosure."

Rafe slowly caught his breath and rose to his feet.

"You really think a shadow cat would attack me just because it was annoyed?" he asked skeptically.

"You can be very annoying Rafe!"

He just rolled his eyes.

His cocky attitude prompted me to add, "I looked it in the eyes, too. It didn't attack me, did it?"

"Really?" he asked skeptically.

I thought of that moment when the shadow cat and I had stared at each other and found a connection that went beyond the need for words. In that moment, I had tapped into the instinct that guides creatures in the wild. It taught me a lesson about nature that weeks of survival training on Mt. Orion had failed to do. It was a profound revelation and not something I thought Rafe would understand or appreciate.

"Of course not. I was just teasing," I lied.

I couldn't tell if his shrug meant he didn't believe me or didn't really care. *He was hard to read sometimes.*

"It's getting late. We should probably head down to the restricted level," he said.

"Restricted?"

"Yeah restricted, but Father's passcode should get us in. Come on."

We travelled silently through the corridors of the Menagerie and down two different stairwells until we came to a metal door equipped with a keypad very similar to the service entrance we had used to enter the facility.

As promised Rafe's stolen code opened the door and I couldn't help but think that any security system which allowed two curious teenagers to roam around at will was not very efficient.

I soon learned the adults of New Athens weren't quite as trusting as they seemed.

The first thing I noticed about this new restricted level was that it had significantly better security. The corridor was crossed at regular intervals by thin narrow beams of light about six inches above floor level. Clearly it was some sort of sensor, which undoubtedly triggered an alarm.

There were also keypads next to each access panel for the enclosures on this level. Even if we could make it down the corridor, unless Rafe's father's code worked on these keypads, we would not be looking at any mythical monsters tonight.

"So how do we get past the security?"

"The MAGS."

"MAGS?"

"**M**enagerie **A**utomated **G**uardian **S**ystem – MAGS."

"You plan to use security bots to get around the security. That's insane."

"No, it's inspired, and it will work. The MAGS like me."

Before I could argue further a large metal ball about 2 feet in diameter came rolling down the corridor towards us. My first instinct was panic – **we had been caught**. Then I notice that the laser detection beams deactivated to allow the robot to pass through. *Interesting*.

If this was one of Rafe's MAGS, perhaps it could help us get into the enclosure with the mythical monster after all.

As the metal ball neared us, it slowed its forward movement and long slender rods shot out of the sphere to form legs and arms.

Another rod rose from the top of the sphere with a tiny camera attached. It looked a little like the eye stalk of a wild Blue Hydra that hunts insects along the shores of Lake Hera.

"This is a restricted area. State your reason for being here," its tinny voice announced.

"It's me, TR-7. Rafe."

For a second the entire ball tilted slightly to the right in a bizarre imitation of a human head deep in thought. It must have been checking its data banks, because it quickly responded.

"You are Rafe. The son of the Director. You are authorized to enter enclosures to feed and care for animals in the Menagerie."

"Correct, TR-7."

"Your clearance does not include the restricted level, Rafe, son of the Director. You are too young to be exposed to the more dangerous creatures kept here."

"I'm not here to feed the animals. Father sent me to retrieve his crystal reader from the Genotec enclosure. He needs some of the data on it right away, but was too busy to come himself. Check the logs. I used his access code to enter this level. That means he gave me permission to be here."

Again, the MAGS sphere tilted slightly to process the new information. It only took a few moments for the little robot to accept Rafe's logic.

"Confirmed. You used the Director's access code to enter restricted level. I will guide you to the enclosure to facilitate your collecting of the Director's crystal reader."

"Thank you, TR-7. That would be very helpful."

Rafe looked over at me with a particularly cocky grin. Normally I rolled my eyes in disgust at such displays, but considering he had just convinced the security robot to get us past the security system, I grinned back.

Rafe was daring and smart, and this security system was seriously flawed.

"Here is the Genotec observation area last accessed by the Director. His crystal reader must be within."

"Thank you, TR-7. Would you wait here to take us back out?"

"Affirmative."

Rafe typed in his stolen code and the Genotec door slid open. After following him inside and waiting for the door to reclose, I whispered, "That was very clever."

"Thank you," he replied with a grin.

"I'm impressed, but there is a problem with your excuse. How are you going to explain it to TR-7, when we come back out without your Father's crystal reader?"

"I won't have to," Rafe said, reaching inside his cloak and pulling out a crystal reader. "Look I just found it."

"You had this planned all along!" I gasped in awe, as I realized Rafe was probably one of the cleverest people I had ever met.

His sister Ardella was smart, but all her intelligence was used in accumulating information. Rafe was able to use knowledge to convince others to do what he wanted them to do and without them even realizing his deception.

I couldn't decide if I was horrified or envious of Rafe's skills at manipulation. It made me suddenly wonder if joining him on this little night adventure had really been my decision.

"It is Father's old crystal reader," he announced, holding up the device for my inspection. "He loaned it to me to use for my classes at the Academy. It will even register as his, if TR-7 wanted to check."

"Amazing," I said truly impressed, even though I could hear my mother's voice in my head telling me his methods were not the Amazon way.

"Let's see what Genotec created this time. Lights up one half level in the enclosure," Rafe announced.

His command revealed that one entire wall of this room was actually made of glass and overlooked the enclosure. This was different than the rest of the Menagerie.

The lights Rafe had called for illuminated a rocky cave with sparse vegetation. At first it looked empty until I noticed a humanoid shaped creature sleeping in the far corner.

Although it was too far to see clearly, I could make out two arms, two legs, a muscular torso and …

My mind was suddenly overcome with terror and grew a little hazy trying to make sense what I was seeing. It couldn't be, could it?

The creature in corner had the horns of a bull protruding from each side of its head.

"Is that what I think it is?" Rafe asked with a similar terror in his voice.

"That's a Minotaur."

Chapter 9
From the journal of Lyessa, princess of the Amazons

The 21st day of the month of Athena
Two thousand six hundred and thirty years Ab Terra Condita

I really am trying to finish my journal entry. This time it was Mistress Claudia who interrupted. I only met her once before, when she came to observe my physical education class playing Triad, but she had a very interesting request.

She wants me to teach her advance girls PE class how to play Triad. She explained that it had always been considered a male sport, but with my help she was going to change that.

I was actually surprised to learn Demetrius hadn't been entirely wrong when he said girls don't play Triad. In New Athens that really seems to be the truth.

But I accepted the challenge, so soon both girls and boys will play Triad in PE at the Academy. *I wonder what my sister Amazons will say?*

So where was I in the story? (I remember – it was the moment I realized I shouldn't have done something so dangerous.)

"That's a Minotaur," I gasped.

"It can't be," Rafe argued. "The Goddess can mutate animals into monsters, but she can't actually make an animal human – or almost human."

"No. The Olympians cannot create human life, but what if she turned a human into an animal?"

"What person would volunteer to be turned into a monster?"

I doubted the poor person within the Minotaur had volunteered to be transformed, but I didn't share that thought with Rafe. His simple, honest question reminded me that despite is cocky attitude, he was only ten and in many ways as innocent as his sister Ardella.

"I wish it wasn't asleep, I would like to get a better look. I wonder if it has the face of a bull or just its horns. Do you think it has hooves or feet?" Rafe began to chatter pacing in front of the glass.

"I'm afraid you would have to go inside the enclosure to learn any of that," I replied in a tone that I meant to be sarcastic – *my mistake*.

"Good idea. Let's go!" he said, heading toward the access panel.

"Wait! I was not suggesting we go inside. That is a Minotaur."

"Yeah!"

"Even if we only go by the stories from classical mythology, the Minotaur is not a monster we should mess with. To top that - this one was created for the Olympics to challenge Arcadia's best fighters. It has to be dangerous."

"And right now it's asleep. I'm not suggesting we wake it up and fight it. I just want a closer look."

"I don't know."

"Come on. We can sneak inside very quietly. If it starts to wake up, we just let go of the panel - like in the shadow cat enclosure. We won't be in any real danger."

"Rafe…"

"Come on, Lyessa. We didn't come all this way and risk getting expelled to watch it sleep from behind some protective glass wall. How many people can say they have been close enough to touch a real live Minotaur?"

"I'll go inside with you, but we aren't touching it," I said with a sigh of defeat. I moved to the access panel and started to touch it when a strange thought occurred to me and I could not hold it in. "Rafe, I know you are manipulating me, so why am I letting you do it?"

He grinned at me. "I'm not manipulating you. I just understand you better than most people. For instance, I'm not asking you to do anything you don't really want to do, am I?"

"Really," I scoffed, trying to sound offended.

He didn't believe me.

"I know you have to act serious and always think about your duty as an Amazon, but deep inside, Lyessa, I think you crave excitement as much as I do. This may be your only chance for a little fun. Do you really want to let it get away?"

A strange warmth filled my chest at his words. Even though I had never really considered the possibility before, my heart knew that he was right. I was a little wild. I had to fight my nature every day to be a good Amazon. *How could he know something about me that I didn't even know about myself.*

To my shame, I didn't worry about rules or Amazon tradition in that moment. I just did what I wanted to do, because I wanted to do it.

"Let's go," I said, placing my hand on the panel.

The brightness of the artificial lights reflected off the stones instinctively caused me to squint, but it was only a few seconds before they adjusted enough to allow me to see Rafe's sudden appearance in the enclosure.

Giving him a chance to adjust to the light, I found myself studying the rock formations, the texture of the stone, and the odd tendrils of red dust swirling along the floor – looking anywhere but in the direction of the sleeping Minotaur. Truth be told, real fear of what I might see was starting to set in and being a wild child was starting to be less appealing than it had been outside the enclosure.

Rafe showed no outward signs of fear, but signaled with his hand that we should move toward where we had seen the Minotaur sleeping. Even Rafe wasn't cocky enough to make any noise that might wake the monster. The Amazon in me appreciated his hunter's instincts.

As we moved closer and closer to the sleeping Minotaur, I watched for any signs that it was waking or might be aware of our presence. It's deformed, yet recognizably human face, remained passive and calm. It was fast asleep.

When Rafe reached out to touch the creature, I caught his hand to stop him. I shook my head trying hard to communicate my objection. *Was he crazy?* Surely touching the Minotaur would wake it, and what would it do if found two silly teenagers sneaking around its enclosure?

Before I could determine if Rafe understood my warning, an ear shattering roar caused every hair on my body to stand on end. Terror froze by limbs. I looked again at the Minotaur in front of me. Although it seemed to be stirring, its eyes were still closed.

"How could it roar in its sleep?" I wondered, until the horrible realization hit me. The sound hadn't come from the sleeping creature. It had come from behind us. There was more than one Minotaur.

"Lyessa, look out!" Rafe cried throwing himself into me hard enough to leave us both sprawling on the ground beside the now waking Minotaur.

I was able to look back over Rafe's shoulder to see the club of the second, bigger Minotaur filling the space my head had occupied only moments earlier. That would have hurt - a lot.

"Lyessa, there is more than one. We have to get out of here."

"Tell me something I haven't already figured out for myself," I grumbled, struggling to my feet to make a run for the door. When I reached back to help Rafe up, Ardella's brother simply disappeared without a trace.

"What?" my terrified brain screeched, until I realized the error I had made in my panic. I didn't have to run anywhere.

"Rafe let go of the panel. He is safely outside the enclosure," I assured myself.

Even as my mind rejoiced at my friend's quick thinking my body was too busy dodging the Minotaur's next swing to follow his lead.   In fact, I found myself stumbling backwards slipping on the loose stone floor of the rocky cave wishing I could come and go from this virtual world as easily as Rafe.

"I have to get out of here. I have to let go of the panel," I told my brain even as my arms were busy reaching for the large branch I had just stumbled upon.

As the Minotaur once again swung his club at my head, I found myself very grateful that my sister Serena had made my Bodan staff training so rigorous. I not only managed to raise the branch to defend against the monstrous blow, but through pure instinct I was able to push him back, swing around, and land a blow on his upper thigh.

The club-wielding Minotaur roared in pain, and stepped away from me. I knew he wasn't really hurt, but hoped that the shock would allow me a few moments to focus and get my real body outside the enclosure to cooperate.

Unfortunately, the sleeping Minotaur was now fully awake and more than a little irritated that I had hit her mate. (Don't ask me how I suddenly knew the first Minotaur was a girl. I just did.)

I watched the subtle change in her posture and the sudden fire in her eyes and realized she was about to charge. Stomping her foot and lowering her head until her deadly horns were even with my face, the female Minotaur let out   scratchy growl and began to move.

I watched in a sort of fascinated terror. I was about to be impaled on its horns, unless I could find a way to stop a raging half-woman, half-bull monster in the next few seconds. *How likely was that?*

"What do you think you are doing?" Rafe cried, as he gripped my arm and yanked me out of the Minotaur's path. I felt the warm rush of air created as the monster rushed past narrowly missing my right arm. I was unharmed – *for now*.

Hope roared to life within my heart as I realized Rafe had come back for me. I didn't have to do this alone. I started to thank him, but he was all about the business of survival.

"Don't fight the Minotaur," he cried. "Let go of the panel, and let's get out of here."

Does he really think I don't already know that?

"I want to, Rafe, but I can't seem to concentrate long enough do it while my body believes it is battling for its life."

"This isn't real," Rafe argued.

"It feels real enough, and the … Look out!"

The club of the now fully recovered male Minotaur swung dangerously close to Rafe's head as the female monster let out a loud bellow that sounded like encouragement for her mate's efforts.

"I will distract them while you concentrate on getting out of here. Try closing your eyes – it helps."

"Rafe, you can't handle both of them at once," I argued, but Ardella's crazy brother was already charging the female Minotaur. *Who in their right mind charges a Minotaur?*

His daring plan seemed to be working as he turned at the last moment and ran directly between the shocked Minotaurs and kept going. Both the Minotaurs turned to watch his retreating form, giving me the opportunity he had promised to concentrate on exiting the enclosure.

I commanded my brain to move my right hand off the panel. Since I could neither see nor feel my real hand out in the observation room, this effort produced very little positive results. I even tried closing my eyes as Rafe suggested, but my hand would not move.

My survival training had taken over to help me fight the Minotaur, but for this situation that was proving to be a problem. My fight or flight response was keeping my logical mind from operating the way it was supposed to.

It was no good. I was trapped inside this enclosure with two angry Minotaurs, but I knew Rafe didn't have to be.

"I can't get out, Rafe. Let go of the panel. Save yourself."

"I'm not leaving here without you, Lyessa," Rafe shouted, as he twisted around and jumped over a low swing of the club. I had seen him use a similar move in our last Triad game – minus the club and the Minotaur, of course.

"Get out of here, then you can pull my hand off the panel."

"That just might work, if we…"

But Rafe never finished his sentence as the Minotaur's club made contact with his back. I heard what sounded like cracking bones and saw the shock and pain on his face before he blinked once and was no longer there.

"By the Goddess, I hope he's alright," I whispered, as I grasped that his painful type of exit would most likely be mine as well. It was one way to escape.

As the female stared at me with a feral gleam in her eyes, I knew she would be charging again soon. This was the end.

I wondered briefly if being impaled on a Minotaur's horns would be more or less painful than my sisters' stories of being impaled by a Harpy's claws.

I came to the conclusion it really didn't want to the answer.

I made a silent vow to the Goddess in that moment. I promised Hera that if I got through this experience unharmed, I would never do something so stupid again.

The Goddess heard me, because as I watched the female Minotaur's horns get closer and closer to goring me, the lights suddenly blinked and I found myself back in the observation room.

Rafe was still holding the hand he had yanked off the panel. He looked pale and frightened – a state I had never seen him in before.

"Are you alright?" he whispered.

"Was I alright?" I wondered.

I was safe, but I would never do anything so STUPID again.

Chapter 10
From the diary of Ardella of New Athens

The 23rd day of the month of Athena
Two thousand six hundred and thirty years Ab Terra Condita

Something is wrong with Lyessa. The other night I awoke to find her missing from our room. She said she had just stepped outside to help clear her head after a nightmare, but I'm not certain I believe her. It has to be more than that. She has been acting moody and withdrawn ever since. She has been writing in her journal every chance she gets, but always closes it when I come in. She has even stopped practicing the Bodan staff with Rafe in the evenings.

It seemed like they weren't speaking to each anymore, until I overheard them arguing just outside our dorm room last night.

"How many times do I have to tell you I'm sorry, Lyessa? I didn't think there would be any harm in looking."

"We did more than look, Rafe. That's the problem."

"It wasn't so bad. No one found out and no one got hurt."

"Have you seen the size of the bruise on your back?"

"That is a small price to pay for the experience of being killed by the Min…"

"Don't say its name. We promised NEVER to say its name again."

"Ok, ok! I promise I won't say its name, if you will stop avoiding me."

"I'm not avoiding you. I've just been busy with other things."

"Like teaching the girls to play Triad?"

"Who told you about that?"

"It's all over the Academy. All the girls are smirking and Demetrius is madder than usual."

"Why is everything at the Academy a contest between boys and girls?"

"You have to stop being so sensitive. It's not just the Academy, Lyessa. Life all over Arcadia is a contest between male and female. It's just part of human nature."

"Is it? I come from a society composed entirely of women, so there is no rivalry."

"I know! I know! Girls in Amazonia can do anything boys can do."

"No, Rafe! Girls can do **everything**, because there are no boys in Amazonia."

There was a silence.

"Remember Rafe, you are the first boy I ever met!"

When Lyessa came into our dorm room, I pretended I hadn't overheard her strange conversation with my brother. It was clear that he talked her into doing something they shouldn't have. At least they didn't get caught.

Rafe's behavior didn't surprise me. My brother always seemed to be looking for a new way to get in trouble. Lyessa was another story. She was always so serious and driven by her duty as an Amazon. She is not the rule-breaker Rafe is, so why did she do it?

At least it sounded like she learned her lesson and won't do it again.   Whatever IT is?

The 25th day of the month of Athena

I sat under the shade of an ancient oak near the library waiting for Lyessa to arrive for our Bodan staff lesson. Looking over at the matching staves lying beside me, I realized she would be longer than I first thought. Fortunately, I always carried my crystal reader in my bag, so I pulled it out and was quickly involved in the next episode of Wonder Woman.

After Mother's work with the comic book in Amazonia, she did an extensive search of Athena's Archive and found many different stories (both books and videos) about Princess Diana of the Amazons. They were fun and silly, and a little addicting.

Wonder Woman had just stopped the bad guy with her magic lasso, when the Triad ball landed splat in the middle of the screen. My heart sank. I didn't even have to look up to know who it belonged to.

"You're supposed to catch it and throw it back, Ardella. Your Amazon friend isn't doing a very good job teaching you girls to play Triad," Demetrius' whining voice announced.

Lyessa wasn't teaching my PE class to play Triad, but I had seen with my own eyes how hard she had been working with the older girls. Although I usually ignored his stupid comments, I couldn't let him belittle my friend's efforts.

"I catch it fine when Lyessa throws its. Maybe you need to work on throwing it correctly."

"Very funny. You're very brave considering your Amazon friend isn't here to defend you. Neither is your brother, is he?"

"I don't need them to defend me."

"That's good, because it seems to me they spend a lot more time together than they do with you. You must be really pathetic to lose your best friend to your brother."

"Go away, Demetrius!"

"No," he gloated.

He knew that he had gotten under my skin. That would only make him keep jabbing that one spot. Rafe had told me the best tactic in this situation was to distract him. I looked down at the Triad ball in my lap and had an idea.

Now I wasn't very good at throwing and catching (Demetrius had been right about that), but I was better in geometry than he was.

Standing I put the crystal reader back in my bag and contemplated the Triad ball in my hands.

"So, I'm supposed to throw it back, right?"

"Yeah."

"So back up and I will give it a try."

"Just toss it to me."

"No. I want to try. Back up and I will pass it to you."

"You're just going to embarrass yourself."

"Let me try."

"Alright. Alright. If it's the only way to get the ball back, then have it your way."

He backed up about 15 feet. It seemed to be a reasonable length for a Triad throw, although a little far for a newbie. He was hoping I would fail.

I thought about the angle necessary and arched it toward Demetrius. The ball didn't go 15 feet. It sailed over his head and landed another 20 feet past him.

"Hey!" he protested, rushing off to retrieve his Triad ball.

"Guess I do need more practice," I shouted at his back.

With that I sat back down and started to pull out my crystal reader, but I had forgotten Demetrius never lets anything go that easily.

"You think that was funny?" he asked, trudging back from where he had found his Triad ball.

I was ready for him. I couldn't shake the bully, so I was going to beat him another way.

"Why are you mad? You were right. I am a terrible at throwing Triad balls."

"But you did that on purpose."

"How could I, if I can't play Triad?"

"You threw it over my head!"

"So, you were wrong? I am a good Triad player?"

"You…"

But suddenly he stopped. I could tell by his intense look of concentration that was trying to figure out the right answer to win this conversation. I smiled. He wouldn't. We had just entered my area of strength. I loved to debate.

"So where are your brother and Lyessa?" Demetrius asked suddenly.

Curious – when he realized he couldn't win the debate, he went right back to the last successful mean thing his little brain had come up with. *So much for distracting Demetrius.*

"I have no idea where Rafe is, but Lyessa is at a rehearsal for her Choral Music class. We have a Bodan staff lesson when she is done."

"Bodan staff?" Demetrius asked in a tone that managed to sound like he was implying I made the word up.

I rolled my eyes and pointed to the two staves lying beside the tree.

"Oh. You mean the stupid Amazon sticks Rafe is always going on about."

"A Bodan staff is a two-thousand-year-old weapon with a long tradition of defending the Amazon nation. It is not a STICK."

"Think about it. It can't really be a weapon, if you can use it, Ardella."

That sounded like what Rafe had once said. That time my best friend had suggested I fight him, but I had declined. Looking back now I realize Lyessa had been trying to boost my confidence and get me to stand up to my brother.

"Goodbye, Ardella. I hope your friend isn't so busy with your brother that she forgets you are waiting," he said, and with that caustic comment turned to go.

I should have just let him go. That is what I had been trying to get him to do since he arrived. The problem is that as I stared down at the Bodan staff and then back up at Demetrius' back, I suddenly didn't want him to go.

"Demetrius!" I shouted.

When he turned, I threw the Bodan staff towards him just as I had once watched Lyessa throw one at Rafe. Like my brother, Demetrius caught it without any problem. (It must be Triad reflexes.)

"What's this?"

"I challenge you to a match."

"If you think I'm fighting you, you're crazy."

"So, you are admitting I can do something you can't?"

"I didn't say I couldn't do it. I said I'm not going to do it."

"So, when I tell everyone you refused my challenge…"

"Tell them I thought it was stupid," he sneered.

But this was still a debate, and I had just won.

"Tell them you were scared I would beat you again like in the History Challenge. Got it!"

"Ardella!" Demetrius growled.

I couldn't help but notice his hands tighten on the Bodan staff and felt a sudden shiver of doubt.

The first-time Demetrius had bullied me I had been too shocked and hurt to react with anything but tears. I didn't understand why he was being so mean, so I had no idea what to do. That day Rafe had handled the bully.

Ever since then my solution has been to avoid him when possible or ignore his comments when he wouldn't let me get away. With Lyessa's arrival at the Academy, however, I now had other choices. If he wouldn't stop, then I would have to stand up to him.

My brain understood what needed to be done, but my heart was not sure I could really do it. Thankfully Demetrius made the next move – before I could back out.

"You just want to do this, so you can fall down crying the first time I tap your stick and claim I hurt you."

I am trying to find the courage to face him and he thinks it is a deception. *Interesting*.

"You think I'm trying to trick you - to get you in trouble?"

"Aren't you? I can see the fear in your eyes, Ardella. You don't really want to fight me."

I thought about that for a moment, and knew he was right. Of course, I didn't want to fight, but I couldn't admit that to him.

"Lyessa says we must face our fears," I said leaning down to pick up my own Bodan staff. "And our bullies."

"I still don't trust you."

I realized he didn't trust me to do the right thing, because that is not what he would do. I found that a little sad.

"I swear by the Goddess that if anyone asks me I will admit that I challenged you and knew I might get hurt in the fight. If I am lying, may Athena strike me down?"

Demetrius stared at me for a long time as if trying to figure out why I was doing this.

"You are starting to sound like your crazy Amazon friend."

"Thank you."

"That wasn't a complement."

"Yes, it was."

"Whatever. You win. So how do we do this?"

"This is the starting position," I said, as I demonstrated the move Lyessa taught me back in Amazonia. "From here you can swing any direction."

"How do I win?"

"You must disarm your opponent or pin them to the ground with your staff, although no hitting in the head is allowed."

"Ok. Who swings first?"

"Since I challenged you, I will let you go first, but after that anyone can swing at any time."

"Let's go," Demetrius said, lining up with me and swinging the Bodan staff into the starting position.

"Ready," I replied, hoping my voice didn't sound as shaking as I felt.

Although I was watching him carefully trying to anticipate his first strike (like Lyessa taught me), the actual force of his staff against mine shocked me and nearly buckled my knees. He hit a lot harder than Lyessa.

He chuckled like he had already won. I had forgotten to bend my knees and elbows to absorb the blow. I was too nervous about facing Demetrius. That had been a stupid mistake.

"This is gonna be too easy," he gloated, swinging the Bodan staff once more toward me.

This time I blocked the blow correctly and took the opportunity to swing back at Demetrius. He blocked my blow, but did look a little shocked that I had actually swung at him.

"Do not be so sure," I suggested, as I stepped backed, and readjusted to the starting position.

"You don't really think you can beat me, do you?" Demetrius laughed, as he swung wide causing me to jump back to avoid being hit in the shoulder.

"I do not care about beating you, Demetrius. I only care about proving I am not scared of you anymore."

"I can still see the fear in your eyes, Ardella. You're never going to prove anything to me like this."

"Forgive me for not being clear, Demetrius. I am not trying to prove to you that I am not scared. I am trying to prove it to myself."

"That's stupid."

"Every blow I strike," I said swinging at his chest. "Will make it that much easier," I added with another swing. "To tell you to leave me alone next time."

The sound of my Bodan staff cracking against his was music to my ears. It cracked the ball of fear in the pit of my stomach that had been controlling me into tiny pieces.

Demetrius frowned at me.

"Just because your crazy Amazon friend taught you to swing a stick, doesn't mean you can fight," he growled and took the offensive.

Suddenly on the defensive, I blocked blow after blow. He was stronger and more aggressive, so it only took a minute for my arms to begin to feel the strain. My grip loosened as the Bodan staff became heavier and heavier, and Demetrius' next blow sent it flying into the grass.

The look on his face wasn't one of success, but suspicion and doubt, and Demetrius still held the staff as if ready to swing again.

Even having disarmed me, the bully doubted his victory. I wondered if his doubts about his own abilities were what drove him to be so obnoxious to others.

"You win," I said with a smile.

I saw the look of doubt change to joy. He actually smiled back at me as he relaxed his stance and lowered his Bodan staff. I recognized insecurity – it was a familiar feeling. He just needed me to acknowledge his victory. I could do that.

Unfortunately, our agreeable moment was all too quickly over.

"What in the name the name of the Goddess to you think you are doing, Demetrius?"

"Headmaster!" he gasped, throwing his staff in the grass beside mine. "I was… We were…"

The fear in his voice made it clear why he couldn't seem to find the words to explain. He had been certain getting him in trouble had been my purpose in challenging him in the first place. From his perspective, his worst fears were coming true.

"I asked him to practice the Bodan staff with me, Headmaster," I said quickly.

"Bodan staff?" the Headmaster asked turning towards me.

I picked up my Bodan staff from the grass and held it out to the Headmaster.

"It is an Amazon fighting staff. Princess Lyessa has been teaching me to use it. I asked Demetrius to practice with me."

I smiled at the shock expression on Demetrius face. He would soon learn that when I swore by Athena's name that I kept my promise.

"You must practice this fighting staff with other girls your own age. Demetrius is bigger and older than you are and as a male has a more aggressive nature. He could hurt you without meaning to. Do you understand?"

"*Not really*," my mind shouted, but I simply murmured, "Yes, Headmaster."

"And as for you, Demetrius, I expected you to know better than to engage in such an unnecessary risk. If I ever hear of you lifting a weapon against another girl at this Academy, you are expelled. Is that clear?"

"Yes, Headmaster," he said, scowling at me.

Great! I stood up to my bully to find peace only to get him in trouble and now have him more upset with me than before.

Chapter 11
From the journal of Lyessa, princess of the Amazons

The 7ˢᵗ day of the month of Poseidon
     Two thousand six hundred and thirty years Ab Terra Condita

Copy of her letter to Princess Anna of Amazonia

Dear Anna,
        How are you doing? I got a letter from Mother the other day, but would love to hear from you as well.
        My studies are going well – especially in Ancient Earth History. I think having the smartest girl in the class as a study partner may have something to do with it. Ardella is a gifted scholar – even by New Athenian standards.
        Besides my classes, I have been very busy lately teaching the girls at the Academy how to play Triad. I still don't understand why everyone believed girls could not play the game. The girls here are quick learners.
        In fact, Mistress Claudia is so excited by their progress that she is arranging an Academy wide tournament. She was almost giddy when she told me it would be the first one both girls and

boys could participate in. Even the adults do it.

I swear by Hera that I do not understand this culture's rivalry between genders!

I can't wait until the Olympic Games here in New Athens next month. Although it will be the first Olympics I have ever attended, that is not why I am so excited. I know I have not been gone from Amazonia that long, but I am homesick. I am really looking forward to seeing you and Serena. I hope Mother comes to the Olympics as well.

Give my love to everyone in Amazonia. See you soon.

Love your sister,
Lyessa

The 10th day of the month of Poseidon

"This is all your fault," Demetrius whined, frowning at me.

"Mistress Claudia arranged the tournament, Demetrius," Rafe argued.

"Yeah, after SHE taught the girls to play Triad."

"So, are you going to forfeit rather than play Triad with girls?" I asked.

"I am not playing Triad with girls," Demetrius said, grimacing at me as if I cared about his stupid tantrum.

"That's too bad. Lyessa has won every Triad game we have played in Physical Education," Rafe added.

"I am so tired of listening to you defend the Amazon. Just kiss her already and get it over with."

"It's not like that. Lyessa and I are just friends," Rafe replied, even as the color rose in his face.

I considered Rafe a friend, too, but the tone of his voice as he said the word implied that friendship was bad thing. I didn't understand why the bully's words had upset him, but I wasn't going to stand for it.

"Demetrius is just being Demetrius. You don't owe him an explanation," I added.

"It's time to decide, Demetrius. It's almost time to sign up for teams," Rafe said.

"But all the teams will be a mix of boys and girls, and we don't even get to pick who we play with. It isn't fair," Demetrius said.

"The professors decided team selection would be random, so everyone has an equal chance to play. How is that not fair?" I asked.

"Demetrius doesn't like it that everyone has an equal chance to win," Rafe said.

"I'm not the only one doesn't like to lose," Demetrius said.

Rafe looked over at me for support, but I just shrugged my shoulders. Demetrius had a good point.

"Hey! I'm tired of this stupid argument. I am going to sign up to play Triad. Who's coming?" Rafe said.

"I'm playing," I replied.

"Well, I'm not," Demetrius growled.

"Then you better run off and find a place in the stands where you can cheer on the winning Triad teams, because you can't win, if you're too scared to play," Rafe gloated.

"I'm not too scared to play. I just don't think it's fair that they are making me play Triad with girls," Demetrius replied.

"I think a few of the girls were a little concerned they would end up on your team. They will be so relieved to hear you aren't playing," Lyessa said.

"Come on, Lyessa. Sign up is about to start," Rafe said.

As I followed him, I couldn't help but hear Demetrius call out, "Good luck, Rafe. You're going to need it."

As we approached the pavilion where Triad players would soon to begin signing up, I noticed there were twice as many boys as girls standing around waiting to play.

"Not all the girls I trained to play Triad are here," I said.

"Just because they like to play Triad, doesn't mean the girls want to compete with the boys in an Academy-wide tournament."

"But why?"

"They are not Amazons, Lyessa. Most of the girls in New Athens are more like Ardella than you. Athletic competitions are not their thing."

"I suppose."

"Lyessa, I'm so glad to see you. I was getting worried," Mistress Claudia called, coming over to hug me.

"I wouldn't miss it," I told her. "I just wish more of the girls we trained had decided to play today."

"I'm very pleased by how many girls have shown up to play Triad. You must remember they are having to go against centuries of tradition. It is not an easy thing," Mistress Claudia said.

"I never thought of it like that," I replied honestly.

"When I first suggested this tournament to the Headmaster, he predicted I was wasting my time, since not a single girl from New Athens would even want to participate in a Triad tournament."

"He said that?"

"He didn't just say it; he actually believed it. I saw the look on his face a few minutes ago, when he realized how many girls were here to play Triad. Even if there was only a one girl playing today, it would be a start."

"All Triad players should line up to begin signing up for the tournament. Remember all team assignments will be random and not based upon skill level or gender," the Headmaster announced.

"I'm not going to be on a team with some girl who doesn't even know how to play," one boy next to me grumbled. "Come on Corey, let's get out of here."

"I'm staying, Marcus. I'm willing to risk it. I mean there is just as much of a chance that the girl who doesn't know how to play will be on the opposing team, right?"

"Come on, Corey. Forget him. Let's get signed up to play Triad," Rafe said.

"Hey, Rafe. I'm glad you are playing. Maybe we will end up on the same team."

"That would be great by me. Have you met Lyessa?"

Suddenly a pair of curious brown eyes were staring up at me excitedly.

"You're the Amazon?" he asked with just a touch of awe in his voice.

I wondered if it was the first time a boy had been happy to meet me.

"Lyessa, this is my friend Coriolanus."

"No. Call me Corey. All my friends call me Corey."

"Nice to meet you, Corey."

"Nice to meet you… Princess Lyessa."

"Please just call me Lyessa."

"Sure, Lyessa. It might be ok to have you on our Triad team, since you not really a girl."

Corey's face turned red, as he realized what he had said.

"I mean you don't play Triad like a girl, since you're an Amazon. That is…"

"Just quit before you get in any deeper," Rafe suggested.

"Yeah, sorry," Corey replied.

Weeks and weeks of this gender rivalry finally got to me, or maybe it was just the inner imp who had goaded me into sneaking into the Menagerie. I couldn't help myself.

"You should know that I trained all the girls who will be playing Triad today. I'm afraid I didn't teach them to play like girls," I informed him, and then leaned in as if to share a profound secret. "I taught them to play like Amazons."

"Woh," he murmured, as he moved off toward the pavilion to sign up.

"What has gotten into you today?" Rafe asked.

"Maybe I am getting sick and tired of this stupid boys versus girls contest!"

"So, you had to go and add to the competition by making up stories that all the girls play like Amazons?"

"Who says it isn't the truth?"

Chapter 12
From the journal of Lyessa, princess of the Amazons

The 11th day of the month of Poseidon
Two thousand six hundred and thirty years Ab Terra Condita

The Triad tournament was a huge success. Once the teams were selected and everyone began to play the game, the whole controversy of boys versus girls seemed to disappear.

I was on a team with Alexander and Theo. We won our first two matches, but lost our third game, so didn't advance to the finals. Rafe ended up on a team with Corey and Lilly. They made it all the way to the final match. Their opponents were Dawna, Orion and Antonius.

I noticed the randomly assigned teams all seem to have two boys and one girl. I guessed Mistress Claudia was making it work out that way.

The final match was an exciting game of Triad, which I will do my best to describe.

The official threw the Triad ball into the air to begin the match. Rafe pushed through Dawna and Orion to grab it and then run around them to get open. Corey called for Rafe to throw, but since both Orion and Antonius were guarding him, Ardella's brother wisely threw it to Lilly.

Although Corey grumbled about Rafe's choice, he quickly ran toward Lilly with Orion in tow. Antonius moved to guard Rafe.

Meanwhile Dawna, who was at least a head taller than Lilly was blocking her view of the other players. I saw the indecision on Lilly's face, and was worried she would panic and throw wildly. It was then that Rafe twisted to get away from Antonius and rushed past Lilly.

Even as the other Triad players continued to focus on Lilly, I realized she had moved the ball behind her back and handed it to Rafe. With a nod to Rafe, Lilly took off running with the entire pack, including Antonius chasing her.

"What is Lilly doing?" Mistress Claudia. "She usually plays so well. If she keeps the ball too much longer, though, the other team will call a penalty and get the first point."

"Lilly doesn't have the ball, Mistress Claudia. Rafe does."

"Are you sure?"

At that moment the buzzer for the first point sounded. There was some grumbling from the crowd about Lilly holding the ball too long, until Rafe lifted the Triad ball to claim the point.

The mood of the crowd changed instantly. There was wild applause for the trick, as the other Triad players on the field looked confused about what had just happened.

"When did she throw Rafe the ball? I didn't see it!" Marcus asked.

"Neither did the other players. Did you see them all chasing her? She didn't even have the ball," Demetrius added.

"Lilly held it behind her back and Rafe grabbed it as he ran by," I informed them.

"You can do that?" Marcus asked.

"The rules say you must pass the ball. It doesn't specify throwing it."

"I'd never heard that. Maybe it would have been ok to play with the girls, since they are using Amazon tricks," Marcus said.

I resisted the urge to roll my eyes and return my focus to the game.

After scoring the first point of the game, Rafe returned the ball to the official who then tossed it to the nearest player of the opposing team – Dawna.

Suddenly everyone was moving. Orion zig-zagged around the field trying to break free of Corey unsuccessfully. Meanwhile Antonius did manage to get around Rafe and called out for Dawna to throw it – which she did.

Unfortunately, just as she threw it, Lilly ran in front of Antonius and managed to hit the ball in midflight. I saw by the disappointed look on her face that she had hope to intercept it, but it was still a good play.

The Triad ball hit the ground with a thud and everyone dove for it.   Orion came up with the ball just as the second buzzer sounded and the score became tied: 1 to 1.

This time the official tossed the Triad ball to Rafe who managed to throw it successfully to Corey. After several dodges and attempts to lose his guard Orion, Corey threw it Rafe's direction. I had seen this play many times before. His fellow Triad players like to throw the ball Rafe's direction and hope he could beat his guard to the prize.

It was not really a very strategic play, although Lyessa had to admit that Rafe got the ball more often than his opponent – or everyone wouldn't keep throwing it his direction.

Luck was with Rafe again. As he dove for the wayward ball and then popped up to his feet again, he held the Triad ball clinched in his right fist.

The crowd roared. Many of them had played Triad both with and against Ardella's brother. They seemed to like to Rafe. He was a favorite of the Academy.

Of course, Antonius and Orion both rushed toward Rafe intending to keep him from capitalizing on his luck, which left Corey open. Without hesitation Rafe wound up his arm and threw the Triad ball in a perfect arch over Antonius and Orion and straight into Corey's hands.

Realizing their mistake, Orion returned to guarding Corey, while Antonius tried to block Rafe. Dawna had guarded Lilly during this entire exchange, but suddenly Lilly ducked around her and ran toward Corey.

Seeing her open, Corey threw the Triad ball to Lilly and then ran away from an irritated Orion. Dawna once again used her superior height to block Lilly from clearly seeing the other two players.

Despite trying again and again to get around Dawna, Lilly could not find an opening to throw the Triad ball. I realized with some trepidation that the fifteen second time limit would soon be up.

"Throw it. Throw it," I murmured, willing her to avoid giving up a point to the other team.

Lilly, realizing her time was almost up, wound up and sent the Triad ball arching over Dawna's head toward the where the other players for both teams would have to fight for control.

The crowd roared with appreciation as Dawna managed to tip the ball just enough to send it flying back behind Lilly. Despite her surprise, Lilly turned to rush towards the ball with Dawna close behind her.

This time being shorter was an advantage. Closer to the ground, Lilly managed to kneel down and grab the ball first. Unfortunately, Dawna couldn't stop her forward momentum and tripped over Lilly.

Leaving Dawna sprawled on the ground, Lilly jumped up and began running towards her teammates. Even without Dawna blocking her, neither Rafe nor Corey could get clear of their guards for her to throw it to them.

Just as Dawna got up and rushed to guard Lilly, the buzzer sounded and the score became 2 to 1. Rafe's team was winning.

Even as the official threw the Triad ball to Antonius, I realized the game would soon be over. Every match in the tournament had been 5 buzzers, so there were only two more points to earn unless someone held the ball to long and earned a penalty point.

I watched as Antonius threw the ball to Orion who then threw it back to Antonius. Rafe tried to intercept both throws without success. When Antonius threw the ball to Dawna, however, Lilly managed to jump in front of her and grab it with her left hand.

Suddenly everyone was moving toward Lilly. I saw the panic on her face. This time she took off running without a plan. Like a deer being chased by a pack of silver lupines, Lilly dodged her opponents again and again, but it was all in vain. She could never get a clear shot to throw the ball to Rafe or Corey, and so the official called a penalty for possessing the ball more than fifteen seconds.

I could see the devastation on her face as she handed the ball to the official and the crowd booed her from the stands.

"Didn't you teach her she couldn't hold the ball for more than fifteen seconds? I thought you were an expert on holding penalties," Demetrius droned from behind me.

I resisted the urge to turn around and slap the smug look I suspected was on his face with that last nasty comment. Instead I concentrated on the game, and was pleased to see Rafe come up to Lilly – especially when I realized he must have said something encouraging, because she smiled.

The official tossed the ball to Dawna, but when she attempted to pass it to Orion, Lilly snatched it in midair. The crowd thundered as Rafe once again ran past her. Half were encouraging the players to go after Rafe and half insisted Lilly still had the ball. Even I wasn't sure this time.

To maintain the confusion Lilly and Rafe took off running in opposite directions. The confusion of the remaining players was priceless. Like the crowd, they were unsure who had the ball.

For Corey it was a good thing. He stood amid the chaos with a big, childish grin adorning his face. He even crossed his arms and shrugged. It didn't matter to him who had the ball. Both Rafe and Lilly were on his team.

Orion, Antonio and Dawna were another story. They looked back and forth between Rafe and Lilly who had now stopped at opposite ends of the playing field. They had to make a decision and had to make it fast, and they could not afford to choose wrong. The next buzzer was about to sound.

"Rafe has it," Orion announced.

"I agree," Antonius said.

"Antonius and I will get him. You go guard the girl," Orion said.

"Her name is Lilly, and you're wrong. Her grin is wider than Corey's. She has the ball," Dawna said, as she headed toward Lilly.

Orion and Antonius ran toward Rafe. Just then the pair took off running towards each other. They totally ignored their guards and ran past them toward Corey who suddenly stopped grinning. I suspected their exchange earlier had set up this play, but I knew that they hadn't gotten a chance to explain it to Corey.

Just as they reached Corey with the opposing team close on their heels, the fourth buzzer sounded. Lilly lifted the Triad ball high in the air and claimed the point. The score was now 3 to 2. Rafe's team was winning with only one buzzer left.

The official waited until the roar of the crowd died down before handing the Triad ball to Orion to continue the game.

Orion passed it to Dawna who then passed it to Antonius despite Corey's tipping it midflight. Rafe and Corey did a good job keeping Antonius from having any chance to pass the Triad ball to Orion. As the fifteen second penalty drew closer and closer, Antonius had no other choice.

He wound up and sent the Triad ball flying in a graceful arch toward Dawna and her guard Lilly. No sooner had the ball left his hand than the final buzzer sounded. This time the crowd was silent while awaiting the outcome.

The rules of Triad stated that if the buzzer sounded while a ball was in midair then the team that caught the ball won the point. If it touched the ground, then the point was lost to both teams.

Since Rafe's team was winning, all Lilly had to do was stop Dawna from catching the Triad ball and they won. I felt a moment of supreme satisfaction as I watched the ball arch toward two girls I had taught to play Triad. No one in the crowd was worried about boys versus girls at this moment. They just watched as the drama of the Triad game unfolded.

Although Dawna was taller, Lilly managed to jump toward the ball actually knocking the older girl out of the way, but the ball seemed to slip through her hands as she hit the ground.

The crowd roared its approval. Rafe's team had won, but I suspected it wasn't over. I was right. Lilly stood up and held the Triad ball over her head. She had managed to catch the ball and earn one more point.

I didn't think it was possible, but the crowd applauded even louder. It was a Triad match that would not soon be forgotten by the students of the Academy.

Chapter 13
From the diary of Ardella of New Athens

The 20th day of the month of Poseidon
Two thousand six hundred and thirty years Ab Terra Condita

It feels like forever since I have had a free moment to write in my journal. Since we are about to take a fifteen day break to attend the Olympic Games, all our professors felt the need to double up our homework to get through more of the curriculum. I love school and learning, but even I am ready for the Olympic break.

Lyessa and Rafe seem to have worked out their issues. At least they have begun their nightly Bodan staff practices in the quad again. They have even begun gathering a crowd. Some of the other students have requested Bodan staff lesson from Lyessa, too.

With Lyessa's encouragement I finally got up the nerve to fight my brother. He didn't hit quite as hard as Demetrius, but in the end the result was the same - he knocked the staff from my hands. Rafe was a surprisingly gracious winner. He even commented that I had fought pretty well, although he didn't add "for a girl" in front of Lyessa.

My best friend is very excited about the upcoming Olympic Games. Both her sisters will be competing for the Amazons. I hope they are in New Athens long enough to visit the Academy and maybe go a museum or lecture. They should see what their sister has been doing.

Lyessa laughed when I suggested Serena or Anna might enjoy a trip to a museum. She told me that she was more scholarly than most other Amazons, including her sisters. They preferred outdoor activities. She did say they might enjoy a walk in the Grove of the Dryads. I guess that will have to do.

I'm not sure why I am worried about what Lyessa's sisters think of New Athens. I suppose it is because my best friend is worried about it. Her sisters' approval means a lot to her. I can only imagine how she feels. I know I want them to be proud of her and all she had done at the Academy, and I am just the best friend.

I am glad Lyessa decided to attend the Academy. She has changed my life. She taught me things I can't learn in books – like standing up for myself.

Even though he still frowns at me most days, Demetrius has stopped saying mean things to me. Unfortunately, that has left him more time and energy to pick on other students at the Academy.

I want to help them, but I am not sure how. I will figure it out. When I grow up someday, I think I would like to be able to help people in trouble. It would be nice to make others happy.

Epilogue

The sun would soon be setting, and the shadow of the oak tree was long and slender. The fading light was no longer sufficient for reading. Ardella closed her book and looked up at where Rafe and Lyessa were still fighting. They both loved the challenge of the Bodan staff and were highly competitive.

The distance bell from the Headmaster's Tower signaled it was time to return to the dorms. As students collecting their things and departed the quad, Ardella joined her best friend and her twin brother.

"Just three more days!" Rafe said with a grin, as he turned and headed toward the boy's dorm.

Lyessa grinned, too, but Ardella just shook her head. She wondered if he was excited there were only three days of classes left or three days until the Olympic Games began. Knowing Rafe, it was probably both.

The story continues:

Gods of Arcadia Origins: Olympics
coming Spring 2018.

For Readers

Learn more about Arcadia by visiting the author's website. Check out the Archive of Athena and take a quiz to learn which Olympian you would follow if you lived on Arcadia.

www.godsofarcadia.com

Any teachers or schools who would like the author to speak to their students or would like to do a fundraiser with the Gods of Arcadia books, please email

magistrastehle@gmail.com

Gratias tibi ago

I would like to thank my youngest daughter, Linda. It was her complaint that she could not read my adult series Gods of Arcadia (because there were too many big words) that led to my writing Gods of Arcadia Origins.

I am proud of my oldest daughter Monica who found the Japanese song for me to use in Mistress Rhianna's lesson.

I would also like to thank my Latin student, Delaney. She has helped me sell books, given me suggestions and feedback on story ideas, and even asked to be a character in Chosen of Hera.

Finally, I would like to thank the students in my JCL who helped me test the rules of Triad just to make sure it could actually be played. Watching you inspired the Triad tournament in the book.

www.ingramcontent.com/pod-product-compliance
Lightning Source LLC
Chambersburg PA
CBHW031309060726

47590CB00003B/1129